THE HOLLYWOOD WIFE

GEMMA EVANS

SCARSDALE PUBLISHING

The Hollywood Wife
Copyright © 2021 Gemma Evans
All rights reserved

ISBN 978-1-953100-23-8

Cover Design by dreams2media

Editor: Rebecca Taverner Coleman

SP

TRADEMARK ACKNOWLEDGEMENTS

Oscars

Screen Actors Guild

Indiana State University

Ponderosa

Lifestyles of the Rich and Famous

Coke

Pabst Blue Ribbon

LAX

Academy Awards

People Magazine

"Angel Eyes" by The Jeff Healy Band

Naproxen

The Thorn Birds by Colleen McCullough

The Three Musketeers by Alexandre Dumas

Vicodin

CODA, Council on Domestic Abuse

All For Love"

ACKNOWLEDGMENTS

Thank you to everyone who has made this book possible. Thank you to Scarsdale Publishing LLC for taking a chance on me and my stories. Thank you Sharona and the entire editing team for making this dream come true for me. You all have no idea how much you mean to me.

To my boys, Owen and Konnor, I love you more than life. Owen, you had to live more of this book than a child should. I love you, and I'm proud of the man you've become despite the trauma I dragged you through.

To my husband, Jeremy who has always been my best friend and biggest fan, I couldn't get through this life without you. You are my heart and soul.

To Donna and Kerri of A Paranormal Chicks podcast, you girls have been with this journey of edits and revisions for months and I just want you to know that your wit and banter and amazing stories were with me every day! Love you guys!

Finally, to anyone who has ever found themselves a survivor of abuse: Hold your head high and remember your worth. Remember we survived what was supposed to kill us.

PROLOGUE

In 1990, I landed in West Hollywood, California, a fresh-faced sixteen-year-old on my own. As I look back at that year, I wonder whether I truly had free choice in the decisions I made. Most importantly, I wonder whether I could have said *no* instead of *yes* to the offer that changed the course of my life. If I'd said no, would I have escaped without the scars that mar my face and soul? Or was I already too emotionally scarred to have resisted the lure of wealth, glamor, and adoration? At the time, having no other role model for marriage and relationships than my parents, I think I feared that my mother's fate would become mine. That fear fueled my determination to do everything within my power to avoid replicating her life.

I was sixteen and largely powerless, so when a dream too good to be true strolled into the diner where I worked, I may have been running from my past as much as I was running into his arms. L.A. was as much a destination as it was its own living, breathing life-force. Hollywood has always been the producer of mainstream culture, but Los Angeles was where the culture was being lived. California was the land of opportunity, and I don't think my story could have unfolded anywhere else. After all, being a Hollywood wife can happen only in the city where dreams are made and sold.

ONE

WHEN I ARRIVED in Hollywood as an innocent sixteen-year-old, the city spoke of possibility and hope. I didn't come with the idea of fame and fortune, of being an actress. I came to live with my older brother Joey while our parents went through a very bitter, nasty divorce.

Our father was a long-time alcoholic, and our mother was a manipulative and overbearing woman. Mom was never satisfied with anything. She could have lived in a house made of gold and she would still find something to complain about.

That included her children. For the most part, Joey could do nothing wrong, and I couldn't do anything right. I had never been the kind of daughter she wanted. I wasn't a girly girl or skinny. I didn't learn how to do makeup until I was in my late teens. Jeans and tee shirts were my signature outfits, and it drove her crazy that I wasn't her perfect little doll. Neither one of my parents really cared about us; they just cared about hurting each other and had perfected that hurt to an art.

Joey had moved to West Hollywood the year before and Indiana was horrible without him. With Joey gone, my parents' screaming matches escalated into Mom having fits of rage. She threw plates and anything else she could reach. Dad screamed and cussed within inches of her face. What followed was a house filled with tension while they glared at each other through stony silence. The temptation to mouth off would overwhelm one of them, usually my mother, and the hell would start all over again. Anytime I left the house, I never knew what fresh hell I would return to.

When Joey lived there, we could endure the destruction of our family together. Once he moved out, our parents descended into a new kind of hell. I knew I had to find a way out, too.

In 1989, as soon as I turned sixteen, my mom gave me permission to drop out of school. I was ecstatic. I hated school. Classmates bullied me for my weight and for my parents' lack of money. Soon after I dropped out of school, my parents started the divorce process, and Joey invited me to come to Hollywood while they figured things out. I jumped on the next available plane.

Joey worked the graveyard shift at a local factory, and I got a job waiting tables at an all-night diner close to our West Hollywood apartment. Back then, West Hollywood was reasonably priced. Most of the housing was rent controlled, but even with that, Joey still had a hard time paying the rent and bills.

By the end of my first month working at the diner, I'd learned that Monday nights were slow nights. Donna, the older, second-shift waitress, took me under her wing, taught me the ropes, and looked out for me. She and I were the only two working the floor that Monday night.

Donna joined me at the beverage station. "You've got one at table ten," she said.

I rolled another set of silverware and sighed. The last

thing I wanted a ten minutes before my shift ended was another table.

I got my notepad and walked over to the table. "Hi there, my name's Rosalie. Can I start you off with something to drink?"

"Just coffee, please," the man said in a voice that could melt sin on a winter's day.

I froze. I knew that voice. I looked down at him. Yes, the dark-haired man sitting in a booth in my section was my all-time favorite actor Samuel Urban. His perfect golden California tan made his skin glisten and stand out against his white button-up shirt. Beads of sweat formed on my forehead. Sam was one of the biggest stars at the time, and I had seen everything he ever made. I was a fangirl long before the phrase was coined.

Heart pounding in my ears, I hurried back to the beverage station. I couldn't believe I was actually waiting on Sam Urban. My heart sank a little as I risked a glance his way. There was my biggest, most lustful celebrity crush sitting in my section, and he hadn't even looked at me.

Was he supposed to? I mean, he was a big-name actor. Was he supposed to notice the waitress taking his order? *Get real*, I told myself. I returned to his table and turned the downturned coffee cup upright and poured his coffee, almost spilling the boiling liquid. I winced inwardly when I realized I had forgotten to ask if he needed cream and sugar.

Idiot, I inwardly cursed, then managed in a calm voice, "Here you go, Mr. Urban. I'm sorry, I forgot to ask if you needed cream or sugar."

"No, thank you, just black for me. And it's just Sam."

I almost fainted when his dark chocolate eyes lifted to meet mine. He had a smile that crossed somewhere between a mischievous child and something reserved only for the bedroom. It took all I had to remember how to speak.

"Have you decided on what you'd like?" I asked.

"Rosalie!" Nick, the owner and my boss, yelled from the open kitchen.

I ignored him.

"I may have." Sam ran his tongue across his bottom lip. Cue swoon.

"Rosalie, now!" Nick bellowed.

I shot him a nasty look and turned back to Sam.

"You go ahead," he said. "I'll be here."

As hard as I tried not to, I giggled and told him I'd be right back. I stomped off toward Nick, making sure to glare at him all the way to the kitchen window.

"What?" I demanded.

"It's ten. Get off my clock," Nick said.

"Oh, come on. For one, I'm not in school so the ten o'clock thing shouldn't even apply to me, and two, I still have a customer."

"Nothing doing. Donna can take over your table that hasn't even put an order in yet. Besides, I promised your brother I would have you on your way home no later than ten. Now, off my clock."

"Fine," I whined.

What complete and utter bullshit. The one time I got to meet my celebrity crush and actually speak to him, and Nick had to ruin it all because he wanted to be a jerk.

Defeated, I walked back to Sam's table. "I'm sorry, Mr. Urban—"

"Sam."

I giggled again. "I'm sorry, Sam, my boss is an ass. Donna will be taking care of you this evening. I'm a huge fan, and it was amazing to get to meet you."

"I'm so sorry to hear that," he said. "I was really looking forward to your serving me."

My face must have gone about ten shades of red. I could only smile like an idiot. "I was, too. I hope you have a nice evening."

Sam stood as I started to turn. "Could I talk you into joining me?"

I'm sorry, did this A-list actor just ask me to join him?

"That is, if you don't have other plans," he said. "I'd very much enjoy the company."

I fought for all I was worth not to hyperventilate. "I would love to. Give me a minute to grab my things and get out of my apron."

Sam flashed a smile. "Absolutely. I'll be right here."

I pinched myself all the way to the break room, where I grabbed my purse. This kind of thing didn't happen to girls like me. I had been heavyset my whole life and lacked self-confidence because of my weight.

What in the hell could he possibly see in my fat ass? He was probably just being nice to a fan. More than likely, he wouldn't even be sitting there when I got back. But he was.

Sam's face lit up when I reached his booth. He stood up as I slid into the booth opposite him. This was really happening.

Once I sat down, I didn't know what to do with myself or what to say, so I reached into my purse and pulled out my cigarettes. My hands shook as I tried and failed to light one. Sam put a steadying hand over mine and flicked his lighter for me.

"Thank you," I murmured.

"You're welcome."

He watched me for a moment, a small smile playing on his lips. "You're not from around here, are you?" he asked. "Your accent gives you away. Let me guess. Illinois?"

That was the first time I had ever heard of an Illinois accent. "Indiana, actually."

"Indianapolis?"

"Terre Haute."

"Ah! Home to Indiana State University," Sam said.

I took a draw on my cigarette and turned my head slightly to blow out the smoke, then said, "I'm impressed. Very few people know where it's at."

Sam shrugged and smiled. My heart hadn't slowed since I realized who he was, and the way his smile played across his lips didn't help. I still didn't know what to say or do with myself.

From the fan magazines I read, I knew Sam was twenty-eight. I tried to keep that fact pushed far away in the back of my mind. Because I was sixteen, I didn't think we'd still be sitting there having a conversation if he knew my age. I was going to enjoy however long this ride lasted.

The way he looked at me made me squirm. I didn't know what to say, where to put my hands, or how to breathe correctly. Small talk wasn't an art I had mastered, but I tried anyway because if I didn't, the silence would drive me nuts.

"I really enjoyed your last movie," I offered. "*A Lover's Scent* was new territory for you."

Sam sat up a little straighter, clearly pleased. "Thank you. And you're right." He winked. "Definitely new territory for me. You're observant."

My cheeks burned. I bit my lower lip and looked down at the table. "I've seen everything you've made probably ten times over."

"Stalker," Sam teased.

I barked a nervous laugh. "Hey! Whose diner did you wander into tonight?"

"A very fortunate last-minute change in plans." Sam ran his tongue over his bottom lip again.

I tried and failed to suppress a shiver.

The light caught his eyes and made them dark pools of honey. "This is a pretty regular spot for me, but this is the first time I've seen you," he said.

"I normally work the lunch and early dinner shift."

"I see. The real question is what is such a pretty thing like you doing here?"

I laughed and raised an eyebrow. "I'm not exactly the actress type, now, am I? I moved out here to be closer to my brother."

Sam nodded. "Any other family out here?"

I stiffened. "No. Our parents are in Indiana."

"That must be hard."

"Not really," I muttered.

Donna brought me a fresh coffee and topped off Sam's cup. The interruption gave me a minute to catch my breath. Sam cocked his head to the side, and his stare bored into me as I caught his gaze. He'd picked up on my shift in body language, almost like he was studying me. The dissent into family matters made me uncomfortable.

"Sore subject, I gather?" He passed the creamer and sugar caddy.

I gave him the briefest of smiles. "We have a difficult relationship with our parents."

He grunted a laugh. "I get that. My mom's a little on the nutty side and Dad, well, Dad was always more of a friend than anything."

"My dad's an alcoholic and my mom just pushes him to drink even more." I concentrated on flavoring my coffee so I didn't have to look at him.

"Did you want some coffee with your cream and sugar?" he joked.

"Better than that black abyss of bitterness you're drinking."

"Hey now," he laughed. "That's my soul you're talking about. But maybe some brighter days are ahead?"

I smiled without shifting my attention away this time.

Sam placed his hand on the table. His fingers didn't quite touch mine. A palpable, electric charge seemed to vibrate between us. Everything in me screamed to either move my hand or hold his. I wasn't brave enough to do either.

I leaned against the booth and sipped my coffee. "My brother's lived here a little over a year. When he got the courage to come out as homosexual, our dad made him leave. I knew for years that Joey was gay, we all did, really, but a gay son was just a little too much for our parents to handle."

Sam's expression softened. "I'm so sorry, that's horrible. I couldn't imagine doing something like that to my child. Your brother couldn't have picked a better spot to settle than West Hollywood."

I laughed. "That exactly what thought when I got here. I didn't realize how big and close the gay community was out here. Joey's made so many friends. For the first time, he has a real support group. Something he didn't have back in Indiana."

I sipped my coffee. Memory of my dad calling Joey a faggot as he kicked him out of the house played like a movie in my head.

Sam changed the subject.

We shared a lot of things in common. We both loved books and many of the same authors. We also liked a lot of the same movies. Sam's favorite, though, was the theater, something I had never experienced. Outside of the college's few drama department productions, a college town like Terre Haute didn't offer much in the way of sophistication.

"You've never seen a theater production?" Sam asked.

I shook my head.

"I'd love to take you some night. When are you off?" he asked.

Did I hear this man right? Had he said he wanted to take me out? My face flushed as I struggled for words. "That would be amazing, and tomorrow is my day off, actually." Luck seemed to keep running on my side.

"Can I ask you something?" Sam said.

"Sure."

"How old are you?"

My heart sank. Here came the handshake and the "It was nice to meet you." There went my fairy tale.

"Eighteen," I lied.

Sam roared with laughter. "Honey, I'm an actor. I read people. It's what I do." He slid his hand across the table and patted my hand. His steady gaze reassured me. "It's okay to tell me. I don't really care. I just want to know what I'm working with."

I stared at the table. "I turn seventeen in December."

He squeezed my hand ever so slightly and rubbed his thumb back and forth across the back of my hand. The sensation of his skin on mine brought my attention back to him. My pulse jumped and, again, all I could do was look at him.

"Can I walk you to your car?" Sam asked.

"I don't drive. I only live a couple of blocks over."

Sam's jaw dropped. "You walk? In this neighborhood? At night?"

I laughed. "Yeah, it's not a big deal. I walked everywhere back home." I didn't see walking as anything but safe. I had been catcalled more times in Indiana than I had been in California. West Hollywood really was one of the nicer areas. Sunset Strip was only a few blocks away, and while a person wouldn't want to be caught there after dark, the diner and my apartment weren't in a bad area.

"Sweetheart, you're not in Indiana anymore. I'll drive you."

I shook my head. "Really, my apartment isn't that far. I don't want to bother you."

"It's not a bother. I'd actually be very happy to take you, and I'm not taking no for an answer."

Sam stood and extended a hand. Being there in that moment with him felt so surreal. I put my hand in his. Warm fingers close around mine as I stood. I knew then and there this might not be a beginning, but this wasn't an ending either.

Sam left Donna a generous tip even though she hadn't charged us for the coffees, then led me to his car, the only nice one in the parking lot.

"A brand new black 1990 Ferrari," Sam said. "Isn't she beautiful?"

I nodded, impressed.

"I have an eye for beautiful things." Sam's eyes gleamed.

A few seconds passed before I realized he wasn't talking about the car. I had never considered myself beautiful. For as long as I could remember my mother had bereted me daily about my weight. The self-hate tends to dig deep and stay. Doing my best to push those old thoughts out of my head, I simply enjoyed the compliment.

Sam opened the passenger door, and I climbed in. He closed my door and circled the car to the driver's side. He got in behind the wheel and I was in heaven.

My normal fifteen-minute walk took less than five minutes by car, leaving me disappointed when we pulled up to my apartment building. Sam shut off the car and faced me. His chocolate brown eyes searched my face. I could have lost myself forever in their depths. A nervous shiver ran up my spine. I looked down at my hands. No one had ever looked at me that way. I couldn't remember ever being observed so intensely.

"I really enjoyed our time together," he said.

"Me, too." Slowly, I brought my eyes back to his. The same intense stare met my gaze. "Thank you so much, Sam. I'm such a huge fan, and tonight was an absolute dream come true."

He smiled, brushed a strand of hair out of my face, and stroked my cheek with his thumb. Then, ever so slowly, he leaned in and kissed me. I froze. Never having experienced more than a peck on the cheek, I had no clue how to respond. My arms felt like weights. My mind swam. Were my lips too close together? Was I too far away from him? Should I run my fingers through his hair?

Sam cupped my face and a wash of goosebumps prickled my arms. I shivered and let his lips lead the way. Every worrying thought drained away as instinct took over. My body on fire, I wrapped my arms around his neck. As a virgin, I didn't know the things that Sam was making my body feel even existed.

After a moment, he slowly pulled away. He kept one hand on my cheek, but I couldn't look at him. My face burned and tears stung my eyes. I studied my hands and picked at my cuticles.

"You've never been kissed like that, have you?" Sam asked softly.

I shook my head. "I've never been kissed, at all. I've never *anything* before."

He gently tilted my chin up until our eyes met. "Then I am honored to have that position. There are so many things I could teach you. I meant what I said at the diner, I really do want to see you again. How about tomorrow night?”

I released the breath I didn't know I'd been holding and flashed a smile. I floated in a dream. Did things like this really happen in real life? My body seemed to hum. I was scared, excited, and ecstatic all at the same time, and I didn't know how to process the thoughts and emotions running rampant through me.

“I would love that.”

“Me, too.”

He kissed me again, and I responded easier and quicker this time. Oh. My. God. I didn't want this to end. I didn't know anything could feel so amazing.

“I don't want to let you go,” Sam said.

I giggled because I could have run away with him in that second without a single regret.

“But I probably better. Can I walk you to your door?” he asked.

I checked the time and realized that my brother had been at work for a while now, so no worries there. “Sure,” I answered.

Sam exited the car, came around to my side, and opened my door. His hand rested on the small of my back as we walked to my apartment.

“Five fifteen, that's me,” I said shyly.

“Pick you up at six tomorrow night?” he said.

I nodded.

Sam leaned in close and backed me against the door. He placed his arms on either side of me and kissed me again. “One last parting kiss,” he whispered in my ear, then drew back. “See you tomorrow.”

“Tomorrow,” I repeated in a breathless voice I barely recognized as my own.

My hands trembled so much that it took three tries to get the key into the lock and open the door. Once inside, I closed the door and leaned against the wood. Holy hell! What in the world just happened?

My skin burned hot and cold at the same time. I didn't understand my body's reaction. Butterflies danced in my stomach, something I had only read about and had never experienced. I pinched myself to make sure I hadn't lost my mind and imagined the whole evening. Things like this just did not happen to girls like me.

I took a shower. When I got in bed, my mind raced, replaying the night's events over and over again. I figured sleep would elude me, but I was out in minutes.

TWO

I woke to two of my favorite scents: coffee and bacon. That meant Joey was home. I jumped up, threw on clothes, and headed into the kitchen.

"She's alive." Joey flashed his trademark, goofy smile. Although he was five years older, he never teased in a mean way.

"Ugh," I grunted.

He poured coffee and handed me a cup as I lit a cigarette. I glanced at the clock on the stove, almost 12:30. I never slept in that late.

"So, you got in late, I heard."

I rolled my eyes. That old hag in 512 must've been peeking out her door. She spied on everyone all the time and told Joey every move I made.

"And with a guy?" Joey raised his eyebrows over his cup.

"Not just any guy, and no, he did not come in."

"Oh?"

"You wouldn't believe me if I told you." I smiled.

"Try me."

I shrugged. "Sam Urban."

"Sam Urban?" He set his cup down. "The actor Sam Urban? The one you're so nuts over?"

I nodded.

Joey laughed. "Bullshit."

"I told you that you wouldn't believe me. Stick around tonight, he'll be here around six. We're going to dinner."

Joey narrowed his eyes. "How old is he?"

I wasn't about to tell Joey that Sam was twelve years older than me. Cool big brother who let me move in at sixteen and pretty much do as I pleased or not, he was still my big brother and was going to act like one.

I shrugged. "Don't mom me, please."

"I don't like this."

"And?"

Joey sighed. "Can you just be careful? You know, don't get pregnant or wind up dead in a ditch somewhere. Mom would be seriously pissed at me."

I rolled my eyes and returned my attention to the coffee and cigarette. A knock at the door startled us both. Miraculously, we weren't late on rent, so neither of us had any idea who it could be. Joey answered the door. A delivery guy thrust a bouquet of bright yellow roses surrounded by delicate baby's breath into Joey's hands and asked him to sign.

My heart fluttered, and I fought to keep the grin off my face. I knew before Joey turned around the flowers were from Sam. Excitement flowed through me. I trembled, waiting for Joey to turn around. I had never been given flowers let alone had them delivered to me.

Joey read the card attached to the bouquet, then just stared at me. I could only smirk.

"Holy shit," he whispered, and handed me the card.

Beautiful flowers for my beautiful girl. Can't wait to see you tonight, Sam.

"You really did bring Sam Urban home last night?" he said.

"Told you so."

Joey gaped.

I laughed. Today was going to be a good day off.

As the day wore on, I grew more and more nervous. Seeing Sam was the only thing I could think about. I had no idea where he planned to take me, so I was unsure of what to wear or how to do my hair and makeup. The only thing dressy I owned was a classic little black dress that made me feel self-conscious. I hated the swell of my stomach and my flabby arms. I was almost in tears by the time Sam knocked on the door, right at six. There was no way I was something he wanted. Not when he was surrounded by some of the most beautiful women in the world.

I opened the door with a trembling hand. Sam, at six-foot-two, towered over my five-foot-two stature. His black hair was perfectly styled, not a single strand out of place.

"Hello, beautiful." He leaned in for a kiss, but Joey, standing in the kitchen, cleared his throat and stopped him short.

Sam's fingers intertwined with mine as I led him into the apartment. "Sam, this is my brother Joey. Joey this is—"

"Sam Urban. Wow, this is an absolute pleasure." Joey, obviously just as starstruck as I had been, stuck out his hand to shake Sam's.

"Nice to meet you." Sam gave Joey's hand a firm pump.

Introductions over, we all stood there in an awkward silence.

Sam finally cleared his throat. "We should really get going if we're going to make our reservations."

"Oh, of course," Joey said. "Don't let me make you guys late. I'm just so honored to meet you. You guys stay out as late as you want. Have a good time."

As Sam and I left the apartment, I caught Joey's eye and shot him a smug, triumphant smile as I closed the door behind me. As Sam and I started down the hallway, he said, "You look amazing."

I tried to meet his eyes but couldn't. "I don't really have anything nice. I hope this is okay."

"You look perfect. We'll take care of the things you don't have later. Tonight, you're all mine."

He sported a dark purple suit that looked amazing on him. Being the center of someone's attention was usually a bad thing in my limited experience, but I was just so happy to be with him. I marveled at the fact that his eyes never left me.

My mother used to tell me that unless I lost weight, put on makeup, and dressed like a girl, I no man would love me. But Sam was looking at me now the same way he'd looked at me last night, when my hair had been up in a ponytail, I'd worn no makeup, and had been dressed in that dreary server uniform.

Sam took me to a fancy looking Italian place called A'Mour. The restaurant was packed, but the low lights with bright red table linens and candles made for a very romantic atmosphere.

The *maître d'* escorted us to a small table in a back corner, and Sam held my chair for me. I was thankful there wasn't more than one fork at the table. Having grown up using chipped, mismatched dinnerware, I would never have successfully navigated a formal dinner. Sam took his seat and ordered a bottle of red wine and two glasses. My heart jumped, and I feared the waiter was going to card me, but he didn't.

Although I rarely got carded, I worried that tonight would

be the night my luck ran out. Apparently, though, as long as I stayed with Sam, rules didn't apply.

Despite the full house, Sam's attention remained focused on me. He gave my hand a quick squeeze. Being there with him didn't feel real. My thoughts spun in my head so fast I couldn't keep up with them. The excitement of this little movie I seemed to be starring in was a wild ride.

My hands shook a little as I held the menu. The menu used traditional Italian spellings. This was definitely not an Americanized Italian restaurant. When the waiter returned to take our order, I shot Sam a helpless look, so he ordered for both of us. Self-consciously, I looked around the restaurant as we waited for the waiter to put our order in and return with our wine.

"Thank you," I whispered after the waiter left.

My face heated and, in my embarrassment, I looked anywhere but at Sam. That hard ball in my stomach knotted. What was I doing here? Did I really think this was something I could pull off?

"Hey," Sam said softly.

His tone brought my eyes to his.

"You're fine. I'm sure this isn't something you're used to."

I emitted a nervous laugh. "Not even close. Back home, going out to dinner meant going to the Ponderosa. Believe it or not, we do have a country club, but it isn't for people like me."

Sam's brows furrowed. "People like you?"

"Poor white trash, if you go by the kids in high school." I had stuck my foot in my mouth and couldn't pull it out. Tears threatened to blur my vision.

"Well, good thing I don't make judgments based on other people's opinions, huh?" He winked.

The knot in my stomach relaxed a little, and I returned

Sam's smile. Determined, I pushed through my nervousness to keep the easy conversation going.

"What about you, Mr. Hollywood? Were fancy, gourmet restaurants common for you growing up?"

Sam sipped his wine and licked his lips. "Pretty much. Dad's a writer and has done fairly well. He's directed a few obscure independent films in the last couple of years. Mom's a painter. She paints these huge, abstract things that make zero sense to me, but she rakes in the money. When I was a kid, we spent summers in New York, and she'd have showings in a lot of the big galleries up there."

"Did you always want to be an actor?"

I couldn't take my eyes off the way the lights played on his face. The soft glow turned his eyes into shimmering pools of dark honey. His full lips turned up slightly at the corners, somewhere between a smirk and a smile that reduced me to a quivering mess.

"I kind of stumbled onto acting in school and was surprisingly good at it. Drama Club was my one and only reason for going to school most days," he said.

That I could understand. A handful of classes and teachers made my high school days bearable.

"I don't know exactly what your home life was like, but for a long time, the drama club and plays were my safe place," Sam said quietly. For a moment, he stared down at the table, then gave me a sad smile.

"My dad's an alcoholic," I said. "Home was nothing but hell and darkness. Especially after Joey admitted he was gay and they kicked him out."

Sam slowly nodded. "Dad took just about anything he could get his hands on, and Mom just wasn't there. She was a very emotionally unavailable mother. I really think she has mental issues. She used to hide when the doorbell rang. There's always been something not quite right with her, but they both insist that she's fine and doesn't need to see someone."

"Was your dad abusive? Mine was mainly just verbal stuff."

Sam shook his head. "No, not at all. My dad's never really been Dad. He was the friend, the cool guy who let me do whatever I wanted. That side came out even more when he was using. He's mostly stopped now. He smokes pot every now and then, but that's about it."

The waiter brought our food. The plates were thick and white with gold edging. The waiter set a plate of shrimp and pasta covered in a thick, creamy white sauce in front of me. I could make out a faint trail of steam as the scent of garlic wafted up to me. The dish looked too pretty to eat. I suppressed a laugh as I spread the red cloth napkin across my lap. This definitely wasn't the kind of meal I was used to.

"What about you?" Sam asked. "What is it you want, my little Rosalie?"

I froze, my fork mid-bite. Hearing Sam call me "my little Rosalie" sent a warm fuzzy sensation coursing through my body.

I realized he was waiting for an answer, and I said, "I don't know, honestly. The only aspiration I had growing up was getting the hell out of that house. I used to daydream about the day when I'd be free, when I wouldn't have to wonder what was waiting on the other side of my front door."

"Oh, honey," Sam whispered.

I couldn't stand the pity in his eyes. I looked at my plate to gather myself and brought my eyes back to him.

"Well." He cleared his throat. His jaw clenched as he dabbed the corners of his lips. "You're free now. You're safe, and you don't have to wonder about that ever again."

Losing myself in the deep velvet pools that were Sam's eyes, I swallowed the lump in my throat. He wrapped his fingers around mine and squeezed. Safe had a new meaning for me with Sam. *Safe* was something real and tangible that I could grab on to and trust.

All my life, I had been suspicious of people. I'd wonder whether they were genuine or if I was being fed whatever line of bullshit would get them what they wanted.

I decided I wasn't going to do that with Sam. He had a career, money, and fame. There was nothing I could offer him that he didn't already have, so what wasn't there to trust? I so badly wanted the love and attention he freely offered. I decided in that moment to throw out any doubts and just trust him.

We fell into a comfortable silence as we ate. Sitting in that dimly lit room with Sam, I didn't feel naïve. I felt like a grown up. Anything that had happened before that moment was a dream I couldn't quite remember.

The waiter refilled our wine and cleared the plates. Doing a quick calculation in my head, I realized this would be my third glass. I liked the pleasant fuzziness in my head. I was floating more than anything.

"Has acting and Hollywood been everything you thought it would be?" I asked.

"Yes and no. I really just wanted to have fun and make movies. I didn't think I'd actually be as big as I am. I think the success tends to go to my head sometimes."

"Really? I don't see that."

"That just proves how good I am," Sam laughed. "I'm kidding. I didn't realize there was so much actual work involved in making a movie. Between preproduction and post-production, a movie can take well over a year to finish. My scenes usually take seven or eight months to finish just on their own. Eventually, I want to direct and produce. I want to have control over the stories I tell. Now, the theater? That's my heart and soul."

As Sam paid the bill my heart swelled. He was so exotic to me. The way he moved and carried himself. Charm oozed from him. I had no real experience to compare him to, but he wasn't anything like the guys back home. Sam held his arm out and I wrapped my hand in his. We left the restaurant and, although I didn't want the night to end, Sam took me home.

Sam held my hand all the way back to my place, a shy and quiet smile playing on his lips.

"It's a shame tonight has to end," he said, perhaps reading my thoughts as he shut off the car in front of my place. "There's something so different about you, Rosalie. Something I can't put my finger on, but I don't want to let you go. You're like fresh air after being under water. The idea of being the first man to show you things, do things for you...I can't explain the way I feel."

My heart began to pound. "But why in the world would you want someone like me? I'm not pretty, I'm fat. You could have any woman you wanted. Why would you want a fat, plain Jane?"

"Don't ever say those things about yourself again," Sam said, his voice sharp. "You are absolutely beautiful. I've wanted you from the moment I laid eyes on you. I want you now, if you'll have me."

"S-Sam..." I stuttered. "Of course. I do..."

"I know this is fast, Rosalie, and I know you're scared, but I promise you, I will love and take care of you. I'll show you. Will you at least let me show you how much you deserve to be loved?"

Tears welled in my eyes. I did not know what it was to be

loved, but I did know that was the only thing I wanted. Someone to just simply love me. How could I say no?

"Okay," I whispered.

Sam pulled me close and kissed me. When he released me, he said, "What time do you work tomorrow?"

"Two in the afternoon until ten."

"I'll be here to pick you up for work. Would that be okay?"

"Sure."

Sam walked me to my door. He hugged me tight and whispered close to my ear, "I'm falling in love with you, Rosalie. I think the thought of someone loving you scares you, but I'm going to show you. That's if you're sure you want me to, because once you're mine, that's it, you're mine. There's no going back."

"I want to," I whispered.

He pulled back. "I'll see you tomorrow."

I went inside on shaky legs. The need that pounded through my body threatened to drown me. If Sam wanted me, then I'd let him have me.

For the next two weeks, Sam drove me to and from work. Most days, he'd sit at the diner during my shift, and we'd go out afterwards. That time together felt like a fairy tale. Sam talked about wanting to marry and have a family, giving his children all the things he never had.

Sam told me how, in his early years, his family moved constantly from one set to another while his dad took any role he was offered. Sam's early education had been with tutors instead of in a classroom.

By the time he reached high school, each of his parents were leading their own lives and doing their own thing without Sam or each other. He finally convinced them to allow him to attend school in L.A., giving them the freedom to do what they pleased without the added responsibility of his being around. They stopped long enough to enroll him and then returned to their own lives.

ONE FRIDAY NIGHT AFTER WORK, Sam took me back to his house, a beautiful, two-story Country French-style home with a detached garage nestled in the Hollywood Hills, a far cry from my West Hollywood neighborhood. Everything from the décor to the furnishings took my breath away.

White oak hardwood floors gleamed throughout the open concept downstairs floor. The living room opened into a massive dining room and family area, and the kitchen looked like it belonged in a restaurant.

A huge sliding glass door in the dining room overlooked a large backyard and a fire pit. Off the living room was a massive staircase that ascended to a small landing, then more stairs that led to four upstairs bedrooms. I'd never seen a house so large or so glamorous.

In the living room, we sat on a white leather sofa in front of the fireplace.

"What do you think?" Sam asked.

"Gorgeous," I exclaimed. "I've been in nice houses before, but I don't think I've ever been in anything as fancy as this. Do you have like maids and a butler?"

He chuckled and shook his head. "I have a lawncare crew that comes once a week and twice a month a cleaning service comes in and washes the walls, and the baseboards and the floors. I'm not here enough to have them come in more than that."

"Fancy," I giggled again taking in the living room.

Feeling his eyes on me I turned back to meet his gaze. Sam stared, eyes intense. Something between hunger and passion burned in that look. In that moment, I could have stared at him forever.

"Rosalie, you understand I love you, don't you?" he asked.

"Yes, Sam. I love you, too." I'd not said that to him before. I had never said that to any man.

"I want you, Rosalie, and only you. I want you here with me. This is your home, now. Let me love you. Let me give you all the things you deserve."

Sam kissed me, and I tangled my hands in his hair. His kisses turned demanding. My head swam. He trailed kisses from my neck to just above the buttons on my blouse. Slowly, he undid each button, peeled off my shirt, and then unhooked my bra. My heart did a flip and embarrassment washed over me. I grabbed for my shirt on the couch beside him.

"Stop that," he whispered. "You are beautiful. I love your body. Please, Rosalie, let me show you I love you."

Sam's lips closed gently over one exposed nipple. Desire streaked through me. I froze. He could have asked for my soul and I would have agreed.

Sam laid me back on the couch and came down on top of me. His weight crushed me into the cushions and felt so right. He continued kissing and stroking me. Fear and wonder held me powerless in his spell. My breath came in short gasps, and my body trembled.

Sam stopped and drew back far enough to meet my gaze. "See, I told you I could show you things."

I moaned a small protest and tried to pull him close again.

"Not here," he whispered.

He stood, grasped my hand and pulled me to my feet. Then he led me upstairs to the bedroom. Gently, he laid me on the bed and unbuttoned my jeans, then pulled them off along with my panties. Panic flared, deeper this time. I clawed at the quilt in an effort to cover my body. Carefully but forcefully, Sam pinned my hands to my sides.

He kissed my stomach and slid his warm mouth down to my inner thighs. His mouth did things to me I didn't know were possible. My climax rolled over me unexpectedly and I cried out as wave after wave washed over me.

Sam covered my trembling body with his and settled between my legs. "I love you," he breathed.

I couldn't speak.

"Is this what you want?" he asked. "There's no going back after tonight. After tonight, you are mine. You are here with me. Is that what you want?"

"Yes."

He reached between my legs and fitted his penis into my opening. "I love you. This will hurt just a little at first, but then it'll be over. You're sure that you'll stay with me?" he asked.

"Yes," I panted.

Slowly, he eased into me then, in one hard thrust, drove deep. A sharp, bright pain stabbed then, as Sam began to move inside me, the discomfort gave way to a pleasant soreness. As Sam reached his climax, he whispered his love for me in my ear. I held on to him for dear life.

Afterward, we spooned, our hands intertwined. Sam held me close.

"You promise?" he asked.

"I swear."

He smiled against my neck. "Tomorrow starts your new life."

"With you?"

"With me. Forever."

My stomach fluttered. I wasn't exactly scared. Maybe apprehensive. Events were happening impossibly fast, but I didn't care. Someone wanted me, and come hell or high water, I was going to stay with him no matter the cost.

I feel asleep sore and happy with Sam's arms wrapped around me. For the first time ever, I felt safe, secure, and loved. I didn't have any idea what dawn would bring, and I didn't care. I had everything I wanted.

THREE

By the time I woke, late morning sunlight bathed the bedroom with a soft glow. I knew I needed to call Joey, but I didn't want to move. Sam pressed against me and kissed my forehead.

"Good morning, beautiful." His sleepy smile was hard to resist.

My stomach knotted. Despite everything Sam had said the night before, we had reached the moment of truth. Did our relationship end or begin here? I wasn't sure I was ready for either option.

Sam's smile fell. "What's wrong?"

I shook my head. I tried to speak, but all that came out was a shaky sob. Too many times in my childhood, I had gone to sleep with everything okay only to wake in the middle of hell. I wasn't sure I could trust anyone or anything yet. I bit my bottom lip, trying not to cry.

"You're worried." It wasn't a question.

I nodded, unable to meet his gaze.

"About what happens next? Oh, Rosalie!" He laughed.

"Honey, I told you last night you're mine now. There's no going back. I thought I explained that."

Yes, he had said that over and over, but repetition didn't mean he was serious.

Sam levered onto his elbow and stroked my face. "Rosalie, there is nothing for you to worry about. You're mine, plain and simple. Why don't we get dressed so you can get your things from Joey's and let the diner know you won't be coming back to work?"

Whoa. My head spun. Plans were happening way faster than I expected. Sam wasn't giving me time to breathe, let alone think. "I can't leave Joey. He needs the financial help."

Sam gave me a small kiss. "No, he doesn't. Everything is all taken care of. I called the apartment manager this morning, and your brother's rent is paid for the remainder of his lease."

I stared. I couldn't believe Sam would do that. Joey stressed over rent every month and, more times than not, payments were still late. I could only imagine my brother's relief.

My stomach clenched. My relationship with Sam was like every romance book and movie I had ever read or seen, but why was he helping me? He didn't know me.

"You don't need a lousy serving job, either," he said. "I can provide for you."

My head hurt. I couldn't form a coherent sentence. I wanted him, of course. How could I not? I just wasn't sure of anything yet. If something is too good to be true, and all that....

I pushed away the uneasiness and chalked up the feeling to inexperience.

"I know this is probably overwhelming, but I promise, I have ensured every way for you to be with me," he said. "Isn't that what you want, Rosalie?"

The whole situation made no sense but, hell, at sixteen,

what does? I wanted so badly to be loved and to have a love that was mine and mine alone.

"Of course, I do," I said finally. I weighed every word so he wouldn't think I had doubts.

Sam released a breath and the tightness around his mouth softened. "As much as I would love to stay in bed all day with you, we have a lot to do, and I'm sure Joey's worried about you."

I nodded. I had never stayed all night with Sam and hadn't left Joey a note. I showered while Sam went downstairs, then I dressed and met him in the kitchen. He had coffee going. I lit a cigarette and dialed Joey's number. Hopefully, he was awake by now.

"What the hell, Rosalie?" he half shouted into the phone. "I was just about to call the police. I've already called every hospital in the city."

"I'm sorry," I said. I was, a little. I explained the short version of what was going on.

"I don't know about all this, Rosalie." Joey's doubt made my stomach twist tighter. "Why would he do all this? Something just doesn't sit right with me."

"Everything will be fine." I projected a lot more confidence than I felt.

"Yeah, well, you should probably call Mom."

"Tell me you didn't," I begged.

"Hey, don't blame me. You're the one who took off and didn't tell me anything. In my defense, I thought you were lying dead somewhere. A la the Black Dahlia."

I sighed and quickly ended the conversation. Sam looked at me over his coffee. His slight smile relaxed me.

I sighed. "I need to call my mother."

"Of course, babe. It'll be okay, I promise." Sam kissed my forehead and walked from the kitchen.

I thought he intended to give me some privacy. Instead, he stopped midway between the kitchen and the dining room. I held my breath. Sam might be able to pull off a lot here in California, but he had never gone up against my mother. She was going to be pissed.

I dialed her number. Her line rang once.

"You better have been lying in a ditch somewhere unable to get to a phone," she growled into the phone.

What the hell was with people today and my lying in a ditch? "Mom—"

"Shut up! Do you have any idea what you've put us through? You are unbelievable, and you, young lady, are on the next flight home."

My heart froze. "No. I'm not. I'm staying." I took a puff off my cigarette trying to steady my rapidly fraying nerves.

"Do you really want to try me, little girl? Your brother told me all about your boyfriend. I assume he knows you're underage?"

"Yes."

"That, my dear, is statutory rape."

"I'll admit to nothing. Your word against his," I snapped.

"What a smartass you've become. Try me, Rosalie. He is twelve years older than you. What *normal* man wants a relationship with a child? You're coming home."

"No, I'm not!" I shouted.

My hand trembled so badly I dropped my cigarette. I would be damned if I would let her ruin this for me like she had everything else in my life. A gentle squeeze to my shoulders caused me to start before I realized Sam stood behind me.

"If you try and make me come home, I will run away and you won't see me until I'm eighteen, if you're lucky," I told my mother in a voice that shook as much with anger as fear.

Silence on the other end of the phone. I couldn't believe it. Rarely did I get one over on my mother. My entire life, she had cowed me into doing what she wanted.

"Do you love him? Or, at least, think that you do?" she finally asked.

My heart twisted a little at how defeated she sounded.

"Yes." *I think so*, I wanted to add but didn't.

"Rosalie, you are too young, far too young. There is so much more out there for you. Please don't throw your life away on the first guy that comes along and pays you the slightest bit of attention."

"I am not budging on this, Mother."

She sighed, and I heard a sharp inhale of breath as she lit a cigarette. "I am not comfortable with any of this."

"Too bad." I was being mean, but I couldn't stop myself.

"I'm not agreeing to any of this. You are going to have to bring him out here before I even consider allowing this. You and he might both want to keep in mind that you can lie your way out of a lot of things, but a date on a birth certificate isn't one of them. So, if you want me to play along, I suggest you two don't fuck with me."

"And you should keep in mind that it's your word against his. I'll talk to Sam and let you know."

From the shakiness in her voice, I knew she had begun to cry. We ended the conversation without either of us saying "I love you." I had made up my mind, and nothing would sway me.

Sam sat down across from me, and I summed up her demands.

"We can go to Indiana, of course," he said. "She's your mother, honey. She's protective and worried. Besides, whatever I have to do to keep you with me, I'll do."

Sam leaned across the table and kissed me. I tried to

release the tension coursing through my body. I mean, this man was risking everything to be with me. Surely, that meant he loved me. At sixteen that made perfect sense. All the books and movies depicted love that way.

Sam arranged for us to fly to Indiana the following day. We took Joey out to lunch and then returned to his place to get my things, which amounted to two boxes of clothes and some pictures.

"We are so going shopping," Sam said when he saw my meager belongings. "I'm not putting you down, sweetheart. You've never had the opportunity I can give you, and it's high time you have all the things that have been denied to you."

We took my uniform into the diner, and I quit. Then we went shopping. All of this was fun and flattering—a dream come true. How could he possibly express his love any clearer? Sam never once looked at a price tag. He chose all my outfits, from underwear to my shoes. He had me fitted for several bras. Everything had to match. He had my hair, nails, and makeup done, but he loved my waist-long, auburn hair and wouldn't let the hairdresser do anything more than cut off the dead ends and put it in a French braid.

I believed him when he said that his lifestyle and the people he was exposed to gave him an advantage I hadn't had, so I didn't object to his choosing everything. After all, he was paying for everything.

By the time we finished, I didn't look like the heavyset, mousey sixteen-year-old I was. I looked like a sophisticated young woman.

I was exhausted by the time we started home, but we had a party to attend that evening. We had enough time to throw the bags in the bedroom and get dressed.

The producer of a movie called *Natural Instincts* was throwing a get together and, because Sam was up for an audition, he needed to go, and he was excited to show me off. Despite my joy at being with him, I was a nervous wreck. I knew I wasn't going to fit in with those people. Sam did his best to reassure me, but nothing loosened the knots in my stomach.

The party was held in the Hollywood Hills at a mansion a short drive from Sam's. The house sat off a private drive and was lit up like Christmas. The neighborhood and house both looked like something out of *Lifestyles of the Rich and Famous*. Valets parked the cars. If I squinted, I could have imagined myself back in the glory days of old Hollywood.

Sam opened my door and wings his arm. I smiled, even though I worried I might be sick, and threaded my arm through his. I was floating on clouds as he led me inside.

The women were beyond beautiful. On their worst day and my best, they put me to shame. I met so many people that my head spun. Most were very nice. A few women stared at me like I was some kind of new humanoid species.

I met Sam's best friend and fellow actor, Holden Rae. Holden was gorgeous, with broad shoulders and shoulder length blond hair. He had several big box office hits and was very well known, as were most of the party goers. I reminded myself that as a grown woman I shouldn't jump up and down and squeal when I met someone.

Sam clapped Holden on the back. "Holden, this is my Rosalie." Sam slid his arm around my waist and pulled me close.

I couldn't keep the smile off my face. "It's so nice to meet you."

Holden took my offered hand and lightly kissed the back of it. Very Clark Gable.

"The pleasure is all mine. Sam did not do you justice."

My face grew hot. I'm pretty sure I blushed all the way to my feet.

We made our way over to the open bar, and Sam ordered drinks. I didn't like the smell or taste of hard alcohol and had no idea what Sam ordered. The drink was awful. I sipped very lightly as he and Holden talked. A few moments passed as I took in the room. Suddenly, Sam's head jerked to the right, and he patted my hand to get my attention.

"That's Dallas Riles, the director," He motioned with his head in the direction of a short, balding man across the room. "Will you be okay if I leave you with Holden for a few minutes?"

"Of course," I said.

Sam kissed my cheek and hurried off. I had no idea what to do or say. I looked down at the drink I held. I played with the cocktail straw and tried to find something to do with my rising anxiety. Thankfully, Holden took mercy on me.

"Sam said you were from Indiana. I was born in Evansville."

"Oh really? I'm from Terre Haute." I was surprised to find anyone from home out here in Hollywood. I began to relax.

"I know exactly where that is. We lived in Evansville until I was ten, then we spent a year in Ohio before my parents brought us out here to start their careers."

"I had no idea you were from the Midwest. I don't feel so alien now." I laughed, so at ease that I took a larger gulp from my glass than intended and choked.

"Not a drinker, I see." Holden laughed.

"No, not really," I wheezed.

"How about a plain Coke?"

"Yes, please."

Holden excused himself and wound through the crowd to

the bar. The nervous, sick feeling immediately returned. I was sure I stuck out like a sore thumb.

"Excuse me?" a pretty young brunette said.

I fought an urge to smooth my dress and smiled.

"You're Sam Urban's date?" she asked.

"Yes. I'm Rosalie." I extended a hand.

She chuckled, and my stomach knotted even tighter. She looked down at my hand and grimaced. I allowed my hand to drop back to my side.

"Well, *Rosalie*, I'm Jennifer," she said.

I stared blankly. She seemed to think that her name should mean something.

"His ex-wife," she said after a few seconds.

"Oh. Nice to meet you."

Holden must have seen us talking because he hurried back. "What the hell do you want?" he demanded of her.

"Oh, calm down. I was just introducing myself. I don't seem to see my darling ex-husband around anywhere." She made a show of scanning the room.

My anxiety sent my heart into an erratic rhythm.

Jennifer shrugged. "Must be off powdering his nose."

I stepped closer to Holden, and he put a protective arm around me.

"Jennifer." The warning note in Holden's tone startled me.

"Oh, are you on babysitting duty?" She gave him a pouty look. "Poor Holden."

I caught sight of Sam as he emerged from a nearby crowd. He reached us an instant later and demanded of Jennifer, "What the hell do you want?"

I inched away from Holden and Sam grasped my hand and eased me slightly behind him.

"Nothing. I just thought I'd give your child plaything some advice." Jennifer's locked eyes with me.

"She's far from a child, and your advice is neither wanted nor needed." Sam spoke in a tone so cold I half-expected to see his breath come out as frost.

Jennifer started past us, then halted and leaned toward me. "Keep in mind, little girl, you're just a plaything, just something for the moment," she hissed.

"Leave before I lose my temper," Sam growled.

Her eyes snapped up to meet his "Or what? I'm not your punching bag anymore." She looked at me. "That's what you're for."

"Jennifer." Sam stepped toward her.

She didn't move. "Don't worry, though. He'll never hit you in the face. Can't have someone knowing."

"You bitch!" Sam shouted.

Jennifer backed up several paces, then blew a kiss at Sam and whirled.

Sam ran a hand through his hair, then looked at me. "Are you okay? I'm sorry about that."

I wasn't okay but I felt the need to pretend I was. "Yeah, I'm fine." My anxiety had reached overdrive. I was on the verge of tears.

"Don't pay any attention to her, Rosalie. She's nuts," Holden said.

Sam snorted. "That's an understatement. You wanna get out of here and go home?"

I nodded.

"Let's go, then. We need to get packed for Indiana tomorrow, anyway." Sam rested his hand on my side and pulled me against him so that he could kiss my forehead.

I inhaled the earthy smell of his cologne and felt safe again with him by my side.

We said our goodbyes and left. I breathed deeply of the night air, thankful to be away from the people. The confrontation with Jennifer had left me nervous and unsure. Green though I may have been, I understood exactly what Jennifer had implied.

I wracked my brain trying to remember details about their divorce. I couldn't remember any references to domestic violence.

Jennifer was also an actress, a B one, at best. The magazines had given heavy schedules and lack of time together as reasons for their divorce. Despite the little alarm bells going off inside my head, I told myself to forget the whole thing. Her warning tried to penetrate my brain, but I wouldn't allow the fear to destroy what little precious security I had.

"Are you sure you're okay?" Sam asked once inside the car.

"Yeah, I'm fine. Just a little tired," I said. "Today has been a busy day."

"That it has," he agreed. "Gonna have a few more ahead of us. I've got the screen test for *Natural Instincts* as soon as we get back. I don't have to do the formal audition, which pretty much means the part is mine."

"That's great," I said.

He glanced at me, then started the car. "Don't let Jennifer upset you. She really is crazy. That's why I divorced her."

"She didn't upset me," I lied.

"Good. I love you, you know."

I smiled. "I love you, too."

We got home, pushed everything off the bed, and made love. All my doubts aside, I truly believed Sam loved me. I had never before been loved like this. Sam constantly told me how beautiful I was and how I meant everything to him.

I quit questioning how fast things were going. I wanted to badly to believe in fairy tales and love at first sight, and Sam was sweet and romantic and couldn't keep his hands off me. He felt like home.

FOUR

I woke before dawn to the aroma of coffee.

Sam must have gotten up in the middle of the night. The boxes and bags we'd left scattered in the bedroom were gone, and a stunning purple dress—along with underwear and heels—had been laid out for me on the chair to the left of the bed.

That's how much he loves me, I told myself, and did a little twirl in front of the mirror.

I showered and dressed then did my makeup and hair before going downstairs.

"Morning," I said, stepping into the kitchen.

Sam wrapped his arms around me and gave me a long kiss. "God, you look gorgeous."

I turned around so he could admire my outfit, a silky, deep purple dress with a plunging neckline, nude hose, and purple stilettos. Perfect for California, but I wondered how the dress would go over in Indiana.

"You're going to have to let me hold onto you while we walk or I'm gonna fall and bust my ass in these shoes," I said.

Sam laughed. "You'll get the hang of them, I promise."

As hard as the heels were to walk in, they made my otherwise short, chubby legs look longer and gave me the illusion of having a figure instead of the round ball I considered myself.

LAX was a giant, crowded, headache, but we got through security quickly and were soon seated on the plane. I dreaded the visit. I knew long before our plane landed that my dad would be on his way to being drunk and my mother would be in a foul mood.

We landed in Indianapolis, rented a car, and drove the seventy-eight miles to Terre Haute. I gave thanks for the hour and a half car ride. We made our way into Terre Haute by early afternoon. Once in town, I guided Sam to my mother's house. Dad sat on the porch with a Pabst Blue Ribbon in hand. My mother quickly emerged from the front door and threw a disgusted look at my dad, and I wondered how long it would be before they started fighting and he left for the small apartment he rented.

Dad unsteadily made his way down the porch steps and wrapped me in a bear hug. Mom stood, arms crossed, a cigarette in one hand, and a scowl on her face. I made introductions. My mother made no move to shake Sam's hand.

"Want a beer, Sam?" Dad asked.

"I'd love one."

"My type of man." Dad clapped Sam on the back and led him inside while Mom and I stayed on the porch.

"Is this really what you want?" she asked.

"Absolutely."

"Why? Why can't you just wait and give yourself time?" she demanded.

"Because I love him. Jesus wept, Mom. Sam's successful. He's made something of himself."

"I don't like him, Rosalie."

"You don't even know him."

"And I don't want to," she replied.

I knew from her tone and attitude; she wouldn't change her mind. "You don't have to," I said coldly.

"I am only allowing this because if I don't, you're still going to do exactly as you want, anyway."

With that, I knew I had won, but I also knew that she was going to make this visit as difficult as possible. We glared at each other until Sam and my dad came back out.

Sam insisted on taking everyone to dinner. In the meantime, we went to my old bedroom, put away our things, and tried to endure the awkward situation.

By the time we left for dinner, I wanted the whole visit to be over. At the restaurant, my mother needled Sam every chance she got, but Sam never took the bait. He remained at ease and polite. My dad got pretty tipsy, and the evening ended with him screaming at my mother to back off Sam.

Sam put his hand on my dad's shoulder. "That's okay, Larry. She's hurt. She thinks I'm stealing her baby."

"That doesn't mean she gets to be a bitch," my dad said.

Sam sat back, crossed his arms, and smiled smugly at my mom.

If my mother's looks could kill, Dad would have dropped dead on the spot.

Sam paid, and we left. Once we got back to my mom's, Dad left, and Sam and I endured an uncomfortable night. For the most part, Mom and Sam ignored each other, but Sam never left my side. I couldn't wait for us to return to California the next day.

The following morning, Mom was up and waiting for us. She made us breakfast in what I hoped was a peace offering. It wasn't.

"I'm going to have my say, and you two are going to sit

there and listen." She pinned Sam with a glare. "I don't like you, Mr. Urban, but I love my daughter. I'm allowing this because she's as headstrong and stubborn as I am. There's no doubt in my mind that you would do everything in your power to enable her even if I forbid her from seeing you."

"I would. I love her. She's mine now," he said with a calm I didn't share.

"You're a prick," she said. "The worst kind. You've got money and you think you're above everyone else. I'll give you one warning, Mr. Urban. If you hurt my daughter, I personally will rip your dick off. Do I make myself clear?"

"Crystal clear," Sam answered in that same cold voice he'd used with Jennifer. Sam excused himself to get our overnight bags.

"Why can't you just be happy for me?" I asked after he left.

"Because you are a child playing a grown-up game, and I'm scared you're going to lose."

"What if I don't? What if you're wrong?" I demanded.

"Then I'll admit I was wrong. But I'm not."

She threw her arms around me so quickly that she startled me. I heard Sam coming downstairs, but she didn't let go of me.

"I love you, Rosalie," she said.

"I love you, too, Mom." I tried hard not to cry.

"No matter what, you can always come back home."

My chest ached. I couldn't remember the last time she had said something nice or displayed any real emotion toward me. Seeing tears in her eyes brought a wave of guilt. For the briefest of moments, I wondered what she had been like at my age.

Had she ever been soft and in love? I only knew her as this hard, formidable mountain that I had fought my entire life. Sam and I walked out to the rental car. Mom silently followed with tears in her eyes. Once I was in the car, she leaned in the window and kissed my cheek.

Her eyes shifted to Sam. "Take care of her and prove me wrong."

"Oh, I intend to," Sam answered.

After promising to call when we got back, we left.

I fought my own tears for several minutes before losing the battle. Sam rested a hand on my leg and let me cry. My hand found his, and he squeezed reassuringly. Finally, my tears slowed to a stop. I was on my way to truly start a new life with Sam.

THE DAY after we returned to California, Sam read for his *Natural Instincts* screen test and won the part hands down. Filming would start a week later.

During the intervening week, Sam put me on his bank account and credit cards. How he did everything with my being underage, I'll never know. Money talks, and out here, it even walks.

Moving in with Sam was overwhelming at first. Sam insisted this was now my house, but I still felt like a guest. I didn't tell him this, but he always seemed to know what was bothering me. He took me shopping for a few things to cement my place in our house.

I knew nothing about decorating and the simple task of picking things out overwhelmed me. Cooking had always been my happy place, so we decided to add my magic to the kitchen. Once my I allowed my nervousness to dissipate, I found joy in our little adventure. By the time we finished, I had new dishes, flatware, serving plates and a standup mixer.

We were always together. We never fought or bickered,

and we enjoyed each other's company. Holden was a huge part of our lives, and most nights he and his flavor of the day joined Sam and me for dinner or whatever we were doing.

When Sam started filming, being alone was a weird adjustment. We had pretty much been together 24/7 for almost a month but, thankfully, his was a local shoot. He left early in the morning, drove to the set, and returned home every night.

After my initial adjustment to Sam's absence, this new chapter became a blissful time. I got up with him in the morning, fixed breakfast, and sent him to work. He was usually home by ten each night, and I had dinner waiting. Everything was great.

We had been together almost three months when, one autumn night in early October, I made dinner and then waited, as I did every night. As ten turned to eleven, then midnight, then one in the morning, I started to panic.

Sam took Pacific Coast Highway to and from the set, and most people know that PCH can be a very dangerous highway. Driving that coastal highway terrified me. At almost two, I got worried enough to call the set. A set assistant took my call.

After I explained who I was and the situation, she informed me that Sam had left the set sometime around five or so. She assured me that if she heard from him, she would have him return my phone call.

I was in tears. My chest hurt. What if he'd had a wreck? He always called if he was going to be late, and he had never left the set that early and not come home. Finally, at almost three in the morning, Sam's car squealed to a stop in the driveway.

Sam stumbled into the house, and I jumped up from the couch.

"Oh, thank God," I said, as he threw his arms around me. I could smell the booze all over him. I was no longer worried or panicked. I was pissed.

"You've been drinking?"

He laughed. "What are you? My mother?"

"What the hell, Sam? You're drunk and you drove home?" I demanded.

"What's with the third degree?" He had an arm around me and held tight as I tried to back away.

"You scared the hell out of me. I thought you had been in an accident."

His expression softened. "Aw, honey. I'm sorry. You were really worried about me?" He kissed my neck.

"Yes. I was terrified. I don't know what I would do if something happened to you," I said as he continued kissing my neck. "I even called the set I was so worried. They said you left around five."

Sam stopped kissing me and raised his head so me could make eye contact. "You called the set?"

The fire that blazed in his eyes belied the whispered question. Even before his grip tightened in my hair, I realized my mistake.

"Are you checking up on me?" he demanded.

"No, Sam. I told you, I was worried." His grip on my hair further tightened. "Ow, you're hurting me." I tried to pull away.

He yanked my hair harder. "Do not ever call the set looking for me! Do you understand me?"

"Ow, please...yes, okay, I understand. I'm s-sorry," I stammered.

He pulled my hair with every word. "Do you have any idea how that looks? You stupid bitch!"

"Stop it! Get off me." I slapped at his arms. Pain radiated through my scalp.

"You're as mouthy as that bitch mother of yours. You need to learn your place."

Sam grabbed me by the arms and shook me. My head rocked back and forth with the violent force. Instant dizziness washed over me. When he finally released me. I stumbled backwards and fell to the carpet.

"You bastard!"

"Really?" He grabbed my arm and yanked me to my feet.

He raised his hand as if to slap me but instead shoved me backwards. I fell onto our glass coffee table. Glass shattered around me. A gash in my left arm oozed blood and other smaller cuts bled tiny streams of blood. Every part of my body hurt.

"I'm going to go cool off. I hope you learned your lesson." He spun and strode out the door.

Sam's car roared to life, then tired squealed and he was gone.

Too stunned to move, I lay there, unable to even cry. Glass and blood were mixed everywhere. My whole body throbbed. Finally, I burst into tears.

Sam hadn't been gone more than ten minutes when a knock sounded at the door and Holden burst in.

"Rosie?" he called. "Sam called me, and I couldn't understand him on the phone." He froze. "Oh my God," Holden whispered.

I cried harder. Holden reached me in three long strides and dropped to a squat. Carefully, he lifted one of my arms and examined the cuts. I yelped.

"Shit, I'm sorry, I'm sorry. What happened? Sam did this?"

I refused to look at or answer him. Blood smeared the wound on my upper right arm. The bleeding had for the most part stopped. The two bigger cuts still oozed a little bit.

"Rosalie, I have to take you to the hospital."

I looked up, horrified. "No, I can't. They'll ask questions."

"Rosalie, you have to go. You need stitches."

"No. Sam will get in trouble."

"Serves him right!" Holden half-shouted. "Look, make something up. I'll keep what happened quiet, I promise, but you have to go."

I knew Holden was right. "You swear you'll keep quiet?"

"Yes, please, let's get you looked at."

"But Sam will be mad if I'm not here when he gets back."

"Screw Sam! I'll handle him."

Reluctantly, I agreed to go. Holden wrapped a towel around the wound on my arm, then bundled me in a blanket and took me to the county hospital. True to his word, he kept the truth quiet. Though civil, the doctor remained detached. The nurse was a little more suspicious however and kept asking me to repeat my story. The gash in my left arm took eight stitches to close while the one in my right took twelve.

Before we left, they did a quick blood test because I couldn't remember the start of my last period and with the pain pills, they needed to rule out pregnancy. I was saved from any more questions from the nurse when a car wreck brought two ambulances screaming into the small ER. In the chaos I was hastily handed my discharge papers and prescription and sent on my way.

The meds did their work, and I couldn't walk straight. Holden carried me into the house. We found Sam waiting in the living room. He had cleaned up the broken glass. I wondered briefly if I would have to pay for that, too.

Holden shot Sam a glare, and said, "I'm taking her upstairs. She can't sleep on the living room sofa," then carried me upstairs with Sam close behind.

Holden laid me on the bed then pulled off my shoes and tossed them onto the carpet. He pulled the covers from beneath me and drew them up to my chin.

He straightened and faced Sam. "I'll be back in a couple of

hours to check on her." He took a step toward Sam. "Touch her again, I'll beat your ass."

Sam started crying. "I won't touch her. I'm so sorry."

"Save the dramatics," Holden snapped. He bent and gave me a peck on the cheek, then shot a glare at Sam as he left.

Sam sank to the floor and crawled over to me. I had never seen someone cry as hard as he did. His whole body shook with sobs. I began to cry. I ran my hand through his hair and made shushing noises.

"I'm so sorry," he choked. Sam laid his head on my chest and bawled.

I tried to comfort him while swimming through the fog of meds. At last, Sam's sobs subsided.

"Get some sleep. I'll get your things packed," he whispered.

I grabbed his arm and fought to sit up. "You're sending me away?"

Sam looked at me confused.

"Please don't send me away. I'm sorry. I won't ever call the set again, just don't send me away." I kept a death grip on his arm.

What the hell was wrong with me? I had stitches in both arms, yet I was the one begging him not to send me away.

"I didn't think you would want to stay," he whispered.

"Of course, I do. I love you. This was my fault."

I really believed Sam's violence against me was my fault. I also refused to go back to my mother battered and with my tail tucked between my legs.

Sam hugged me and started crying again. "I love you, Rosalie. I'm so sorry. I swear to God, it will never happen again."

As far as I was concerned, the situation was over. Sam made a pallet on the floor and slept next to me.

The pain meds pulled me in and out of sleep most of the following afternoon. When I finally woke up enough to realize I needed to pee, afternoon sun streamed in through the window and Holden sat on the chair near the bed.

"Hi there, sleeping beauty," he said.

"Hi," I croaked, and tried to sit up.

Holden got up and helped me. Sam came in with a cup of coffee and my cigarettes.

"Thank you," I said.

Sam helped me to my feet. I made the short trip to the bathroom and back by myself. I didn't understand how the wounds on my arms made my whole body sore but everything on me radiated an achy, broken pain. The tension in the air told me Sam and Holden had been arguing. The phone rang and Sam answered, then handed the cordless set to me.

"Miss Harris?" a woman said. "This is Karen at L.A. County Hospital."

"Yes?" I said, recalling the false name I'd given at the ER. My heart caught in my throat.

"The doctor did some blood work last night during your emergency room visit, and we just got your results back. Congratulations, Miss Harris, you're pregnant. If you don't already have a family doctor, we would be happy to help you find one."

I was too stunned feel anything but surprise. "Uh-thank you," I managed in a whisper "That's okay." I handed the handset to Sam.

He replaced the receiver on the base and exchanged a look with Holden.

I reflexively placed a hand over my stomach. "I'm pregnant," I said.

Holden's head snapped in Sam's direction, then he looked back at me and said, "Congratulations, honey." He leveled a hard gaze on Sam and said, "Touch her now, with this, and I'll cut your dick off."

Fresh tears welled in Sam's eyes. "Never again." He sat on the bed and kissed me.

Holden squeezed my hand and left.

Sam called his family doctor and was able to get us an appointment with an obstetrician the following afternoon.

The doctor only briefly questioned my injuries. My heart pounded while retold the bullshit story about tripping and falling into the glass table. I kept eye contact with the doctor and didn't let fear enter into my voice.

I couldn't recall when my last period had been. They had never been regular, and Sam and I had been having sex regularly for months. The exam showed that I was right at two months. Sam and I both cried.

THAT TWENTY-FOUR-HOUR PERIOD, from the time of our blow up, to the ER to the doctor's appointment that confirmed I was pregnant, was one of the most exhausting roller coaster rides of my life.

"Wow," Sam said once we were in the car. "I'm going to be a daddy. I love you so much, Rosalie."

His worries seemed to have vanished.

"Sam?" I was only slightly nervous about what I needed to say. I was carrying his child. I figured I was pretty safe. "This"—I held out my arms—"can never happen again."

He shook his head. "Never. I swear. I don't even know why I did that. I hate myself for what I did. No more drinking, either. I promise."

I believed that we could forget the whole incident and didn't press him further. The life growing inside me was worth

any discomfort, including that trip to the ER. Sam and I would
be okay.

FIVE

I DIDN'T SMOKE another cigarette or take another pain pill. When I decreed no smoking in the house, Sam wholeheartedly agreed and got rid of my cigarettes. Life was good. I had everything I ever wanted.

Sam told his parents about the baby and invited them over the following weekend for a barbecue. He also called his director, Dallas Riles, to share the news and arrange his filming schedule around doctor appointments. Dallas Riles was one of the biggest directors in the business because he was so family oriented with his actors. Families always came before the movie. Dallas was thrilled for us.

Although Sam telephoned family and coworkers, I couldn't bring myself to call my mother. I had no idea how she was going to react, and I was in no mood for a fight. I was a nervous wreck about being pregnant even though Sam doted on me. I worried about anything I ate or didn't eat, if I was eating too much or not enough. The prospect of meeting Sam's parents especially set me on edge.

I still had stitches in my arms. I wasn't nearly as sore but I didn't want to have to explain the bandages. I wore a tank top and an unbuttoned long-sleeved shirt. I had been very careful about making sure no one saw anything.

My first impression of my future mother-in-law was that she was nuts.

Cassandra was in her early fifties. She showed up to the barbecue in a green pantsuit with a peacock feather design, a long, flowing scarf, and something on her head that resembled a turban. Bill, Sam's dad, wore an old t-shirt and jeans.

At best, I can describe Cassandra as eccentric. I preferred psycho. She fawned over Sam like he was three years old instead of twenty-eight. She was dramatic and loud. Sam never had and never would do anything wrong in her eyes. He was perfect.

Instead of knocking when they arrived, Cassandra swung the front door open and threw her arms in the air and sang loudly, "Sammy! Where's my darling boy?"

Sam's dad's face reddened in embarrassment and he elbowed Cassandra in the ribs. "Can't you be normal and contain yourself? Just for a little while?"

"You're always trying to snuff out my little light," she screeched.

"Oh, Jesus," Sam muttered.

"Stop smothering me." Cassandra glared at Bill as she tossed her scarf over her shoulder dramatically.

"Mom, Dad. I'm so glad you guys could make it," Sam's voice boomed over Cassandra's.

"My boy! There's my sweet angel." She threw her arms around Sam's neck and squeezed.

The scene was almost comical. They literally lived half an hour across town and she acted like they'd been apart for years. Then her eyes narrowed in on me.

She released Sam and approached me. "This must be

Rosalie. Ah my dear, you're taking my son. He won't need me as much now that he has you and your growing child."

Her eyes were wide and wild as she wrapped me in a hug. I couldn't pull away fast enough. Her dramatic entrance and exaggerated expressions of love showered upon Sam helped me understand why that was Sam had described her on our first date.

"Oh, stop that. I'll always need my mom," Sam said. He winked at me as he took her by the shoulders and directed her outside where we had the grill warming up.

Bill was over the moon at being a grandpa. Cassandra, on the other hand, wasn't. She insisted that our baby wouldn't call her "grandma," as she was far too young to be a grandmother. I rolled my eyes so far back in my head I think I saw my brain. That barbecue was the longest four hours of my life. I don't think I've ever been so glad for someone to leave.

"Dad adores you," Sam said as he helped me clean up.

"Your dad's funny. Your mother, is, well…"

"Psychotic?" Sam offered.

"I was going to say 'different.'"

"No. She's psychotic."

I didn't argue.

MY DAD and Joey were excited by the news of the baby. Uplifted by their positive reactions, I finally broke down and called my mother. She assured me that she was happy, although I could tell she chose her words carefully. I didn't mind her restraint because telling her had been the hardest part, and finally that was over.

Two weeks later, Sam booked a party at A'Mour, the

restaurant he'd taken me to on our first date, so he could make an official announcement to his friends and actor family.

My stitches were out but the cuts were still visible. I took care to wear a long sleeve dress to make sure the scars were covered.

At the end of dinner, dessert arrived on little trays with beautiful golden domes. Sam stood, presenting such a handsome vision in his dark purple suit that I knew I would never forget that moment as long as I lived.

His eyes shone with unshed tears when he lifted the dome off my tray. Instead of a plate, a black velvet ring box lay cradled in a beautiful rectangle-cut ruby surrounded by diamonds. In comparison to the ring, the card beside it was unassuming, but its message was just as important. Two words: *Marry me?* in Sam's handwriting.

Sam got down on one knee and took my hands in his. "Rosalie, these last few months with you have been the happiest of my life. The moment I saw you, my heart knew you were the one. I've searched for you my whole life. Cliché as this sounds, it was absolutely love at first sight. I fall more in love with you every day. Will you share your life with me?"

I cried so hard I couldn't answer him and only nodded. The entire restaurant erupted with applause. Sam stood and pulled me into his arms.

"Thank you," he whispered. "Thank you for staying with me."

I was ecstatic. Nothing could dampen my happiness. While Sam wanted to marry as soon as possible in the biggest wedding possible, I wanted nothing to do with a huge ceremony or a bunch of people. I just wanted Sam.

When I told him as much, Sam said, "Absolutely not. You deserve the kind of fairytale wedding every woman dreams about."

When Sam made up his mind, there was no point in arguing. We slept late the next morning. In the light of a new day, the afterglow of Sam's proposal began to wear off. I could only think of all the planning that had to be done in a very short amount of time and all the problems that were bound to arise.

Sam handed me a cup of coffee and took a seat across from me at the table. The wedding's biggest problem glared brighter than the morning sun. I was sixteen. California law demanded that both my parents' consent.

"What about my parents?" I asked Sam. "I'm not sure how you're going to get my mom to sign the papers."

"All taken care of. You don't need either of their signatures." Sam smiled over the rim of his mug.

"I don't understand." I was a minor. How could I not need their permission?

Sam rose and pulled a manila envelope from atop the fridge. With an anticipatory look, he handed the heavy envelope to me. I opened the flap and withdrew a stack of official-looking papers. I had to read the top page twice before I understood what the document represented. I held emancipation papers. As of a week ago, I was legally an adult.

What the hell? "I still don't understand."

Sam playfully rolled his eyes. "I had you emancipated, with the help of your dad."

Again, *what the hell?*

"Your dad and I talked about it, and we decided that this was the best option."

The idea of my mother having absolutely no say in my life was euphoric, but I was bothered that no one had bothered to ask my opinion.

"What's the matter?" Sam urged. He had this way of turning his chocolate brown eyes into pools of sadness that could bring me to my knees. "Aren't you relieved?"

"Of course, I am," I lied. "I'm just shocked. How did you guys pull this off? Especially with my mom. And I never had to go to a hearing or anything?"

Sam smiled broadly, clearly pleased with himself. "Well, your dad took care of your mom, and our lawyer took care of the hearing."

"Explain," I said.

After we got back from Indiana, I called your dad and we talked about you and me. Your mother is a bitter bitch, and we both agreed she probably isn't going to let you and I go on much longer without a fight. Your dad agrees that you'll have the best life with me."

"So how did he get Mom to go along?" I asked.

"He told her the paperwork she was signing was to get the final hearing for their divorce."

"He tricked her?" I said in disbelief.

My dad had stalled their divorce for over a year. Apparently, Sam's lawyer had the emancipation paperwork drawn up and sent to my dad. Dad then convinced my mom the papers she was signing were their divorce papers. After she signed them, Dad sent the papers back to Sam's lawyer, who handled the situation from there.

"She's going to be so pissed," I said.

Sam shrugged. "Nothing she can do now. The hearing was a month ago, and she didn't show to contest anything."

I stared. "Did you go to the hearing?"

A slow, sly smile spread across his face. "I went on your behalf. I wanted to surprise you. You're happy, aren't you?"

Maybe there was happiness in there somewhere, a kernel of relief that I may feel later, but I couldn't get past the frustration—and anger. "That's just a lot to take in at one time," I said, smoothing the strain from my voice.

His expression relaxed.

Calm down, I told myself. *He loves you, and he only did things this way so we could be together.*

I accepted that, but I didn't like it. Maybe the pregnancy hormones made me overly sensitive, but I felt like a pawn.

Regardless of how I felt about his methods, Sam had resolved the biggest obstacle to our marriage. The next obstacle was the location of our ceremony. I wanted to be married in a church. I was raised Catholic and, while my mass attendance had slipped, my faith was still extremely important to me. Sam was a devout atheist.

"I would like to get married in the Catholic church," I said.

"Okay. Not a problem. Whatever makes you happy."

"I don't know if we'll be able to, though. There're rules and steps before you can get married in the church."

"Little Rosalie, you just leave all that to me. I'll take care of it."

At this point, I had no doubt that Sam would do just that.

We applied for our marriage license and then went wedding shopping.

WE SET our date for the day before Thanksgiving, making me right around fifteen weeks pregnant and being on the heavier side I wasn't showing yet. My shape had rounded out more but you couldn't look at me and know for sure I was pregnant. Although my dad already knew, I still needed to call my mother. One afternoon while Joey was visiting, I tried bribing him to call her.

"Nothing doing. Mom's still pissed at me for letting you go on your first date with him." Joey nodded at Sam. "No offense, Sam, but she hated you long before now. But you and Dad going behind her back to have Rosalie emancipated? And on top of that you guys are going to call her and tell her? She's really going to hate you now."

"Eh." Sam shrugged.

"When are you going to tell her?" Joey asked me.

"The sooner the better." I grabbed the cordless phone from the couch side table.

Joey leaned toward me. "I want to listen."

"No. If you can't be the sacrifice to appease her, then you sure as hell don't get to watch the show," I snapped.

"Oh, come on."

"No."

"Fine," Joey whined. "I gotta get ready for work anyway, but I want details."

I glared at my brother.

"I'll record it for you," Sam joked.

"See." Joey started toward the front door. "That's why I like him more than you."

With my free hand, I grabbed a pillow off the couch and threw it at Joey. The pillow missed his head by a wide margin. "Get out, go to work."

Sam laughed, and Joey left. I bit the bullet and called my mom.

"Like hell you are," was her response to the news. "I have let this go on long enough, Rosalie. I won't let you completely ruin your life. You're sixteen and cannot legally get married without my consent."

This wasn't the way I wanted to reveal my new legal status, but she'd painted me into a corner. "Actually, I don't need your consent. Daddy emancipated me. As far as the State of California is concerned, I'm an adult and free to make my own choices."

"Bullshit! I would have had to sign something." The choke in her voice told me she wasn't so sure.

"But you did."

"I did not!" she roared.

I jerked the phone away from my ear.

"The only thing I've signed were my final hearing—" She stuttered to a stop. "That bastard! You knew about this, Rosalie?"

"No, actually I only found out when Sam gave me the papers."

"Of course, he had something to do with this. Put him on the phone—now."

I held the phone out to Sam. "She demands to speak to you. You don't have to."

"Oh, but I want to," Sam said in a sweet voice. The look on his face was anything but sweet.

He took the phone. "Yes, dearest soon-to-be-mother-in-law? How may I be of service?"

I knew she was screaming because I could hear her and Sam winced and took the phone away from his ear.

"All right, Janet, you've had your say, now I'll have mine. It's time you stopped being such a bitch to me. The emancipation is a done deal. You didn't show up to the hearing to contest anything. It's not my problem if you didn't receive a notice. Your daughter and I are getting married in three and a half weeks. I suggest you show up, support her, and make this as stress-free as possible for her. Otherwise, I'll make sure you never again have any contact with Rosalie or your grandchild." Sam smiled triumphantly at me.

I bit my lower lip. My mom was a shrew and had done some really messed up things, but I would never cut ties with her or keep her grandchild from her.

"Janet, you don't have the finances to fight me. This is a done deal. You lost. Here's Rosalie." Sam handed me the phone.

"Mom...."

"I can't talk to you right now, Rosalie. I'll call you in a few days," she said in a choked voice.

"Are you at least coming?" I tried to keep the panic out of my voice, but didn't succeed.

"I honestly don't know. I need time. I love you." She hung up.

I felt guilty. Sam had gone too far, but she had cornered him into being mean.

MY GUILT quickly took a back seat to the wedding planning. Three weeks to plan a huge, glamorous wedding may as well have been three days and stressed me beyond words. Sam made all the decisions, and I let him. The wedding certainly wasn't what I would have designed, but at that point, I just wanted it over with.

Sam hired professional planners, who took care of the church and reception. My dress was the only choice I made. It was a princess ball gown with a cathedral train. The ten-foot train was spotted with delicate three-dimensional flower appliques, and the corseted bodice was covered in real pearls.

When I informed the wedding planners that I loved vintage style, they set our theme to "old Hollywood glamour." My dress fit perfectly into the fantasy of beautiful starlets that would soon be my reality. Even I had to admit that I looked stunning.

Holden would be Sam's best man. I had no close female relatives or friends, so Julia Elliot, Sam's *Natural Instincts* co-star, happily agreed to be my maid of honor. Sam still had a month of filming left on the movie, so our honeymoon would be postponed until the end of December.

True to his word, Sam and the planners were able to secure a church and a priest. A week before the wedding, we met with Father Philip, a kind, young priest with a lovely smile. Like many before him, he completely fell under Sam's charm.

Father Philip's parish was a small one located in the heart of downtown Los Angeles. He agreed to a condensed version of the Catholic wedding preparations. Instead of the normal required counseling and marriage classes, we only had to attend two sessions with the Father, one separately and one together.

Sam's first marriage was either never mentioned or Sam lied to the priest in their initial conversation. We each had to go to confession. For my "sin" of pre-marital sex, I was given a hundred Hail Mary's. Our marriage would be blessed by the church.

Three days before the wedding, my mother called to say that she would be coming. Sam flew both her and my dad out to California.

After we officially announced our engagement to the press, our wedding made every headline in the gossip magazines. We were followed and photographed everywhere we went. Sam even planned on allowing photographers from the more popular magazines to cover the wedding and reception.

Reporters wanted interviews with me, but I wanted nothing to do with the media. So, Sam spoke in the interviews while I remained next to him and smiled for the cameras. My age was brought up numerous times, but the emancipation made the underage questions irrelevant.

The constant barrage of interviews and questions and last minute planning further frazzled my nerves. Between that and the morning sickness, I could hardly keep down any food. My doctor assured me that now that I was in the second trimester the nausea should begin to lessen. This baby did not seem to get that memo.

The night before our wedding, we held our rehearsal dinner at A'Mour's. There I got to meet Holden's parents and his sister, Vicky. I tried so hard to keep the nervous flutters to a minimum, but nothing worked. I played hostess and made my way around the banquet room we'd rented and tried to keep my eye on any potential problems between the two sets of parents. I was on my third pass through everyone when Holden stopped me.

"Rosalie, I'd like you to meet my parents, Louise and Sydney Rae."

Sydney was a well-known actor and even though I knew he was Holden's father his celebrity still smacked me right in the face when I shook his hand.

"Congratulations, my dear. Sam is a fine young man."

"We are so happy for you two," Louise injected. "We practically raised Sam through his teen years so this is like watching my own child get married. Thank you for letting us be a part of your special day."

"Thank you for coming," I stammered.

"This is my sister, Vicky," Holden went on.

"I didn't know you had a sister." I took in the petite brunette. "It's so nice to meet you."

"He doesn't talk much about me." She lifted her wine glass in salute, took a hearty gulp, then added, "He's afraid I'll steal his spotlight." Vicky winked and jabbed Holden in the ribs.

"As if," Holden grumbled.

"Actually, I live in London so I'm not here that often. I come back to the States a couple times a year. I hope you don't mind an extra person being here. My brother insisted that I meet you." Vicky's eyes twinkled at Holden as his face reddened.

I smiled. "I don't mind at all. We think the world of Holden, he's become my best friend out here."

"Marrying Sam, you'll certainly need a friend," Vicky muttered into her wine glass.

"Okay, that's enough alcohol for you," Holden nervously laughed as he pulled her glass away. "Forgive her, she and Sam aren't the best of friends."

Vicky shrugged. "Not particularly, but I very much like you, Rosalie. We'll be best friends. Next time I'm out here we'll get together, without Holden and Sam."

I liked Vicky immediately. She was unapologetically herself.

I glanced around the room and noticed my parents standing next to each other, talking in hushed tones and irritated hand movements. I excused myself from Holden and Vicky and walked over.

As soon as they saw me, they stopped talking and glared at each other. "Please, not here and not tonight," I growled. I didn't wait for a response but instead sought out Sam to get the rehearsal going.

A normal rehearsal dinner is suppose to last forty-five minutes maybe an hour tops. Mine lasted three hours. I was thankful to finally go home.

On my wedding day, more than a thousand people packed the church. As my dad walked me down the aisle, I didn't recognize a single face among the guests sitting in the pews, except for my mother and my brother. I blinked, and the priest pronounced us man and wife.

I was officially Mrs. Samuel Urban.

At the reception, even more guests arrived. Sam and I

posed for what felt like a thousand pictures throughout the night. Every few minutes, I was asked to pose for a photograph with a stranger. I didn't realize just how little time I would have to enjoy my own wedding. My mother and Sam ignored each other. I had worried that she would make a scene during the ceremony, but she had only looked sad. Both she and my dad would join us for our first Thanksgiving then fly back to Indiana the day after.

My parents left on Black Friday, and the following Monday Sam resumed filming. Life returned to normal, and the world kept spinning. My body continued to change with my pregnancy. I battled morning, noon and night sickness. My breasts hurt all the time, as my belly grew and became more round the less things I fit into, which screwed with my already fragile self-esteem. Our first Christmas together was ideal although it lacked our usual Indiana snow. Sam bought me a pink SUV and started teaching me how to drive. On December twenty-second, I turned seventeen.

Our postponed honeymoon turned out to be two glorious weeks in Italy. Sam remained loving and affectionate throughout my riotous pregnancy hormones. He even took me to the Vatican. I couldn't have imagined anything better if I had tried.

SIX

IN JANUARY, we had the Oscars and the Screen Actors' Guild award shows to attend. At the Screen Actors' Guild awards Sam was nominated for a supporting actor role in *A Lover's Scent*, which he'd finished before we started dating.

As a kid, I had always watched the award shows on TV, and now I was attending one in real life on the arm of my Prince Charming. My body tingled with excitement at the thought of walking the red carpet with Sam. The media ate up my pregnancy and anytime they could snap pictures of my growing belly they did.

By this time, I was six months pregnant, and I felt huge. Sam assured me that I looked beautiful. He had a custom ball gown made for me, a long, flowing dress of gold satin. I felt like a princess.

Sam hurried all over the house as he dressed for the show, a ball of nervous excitement himself. *A Lover's Scent* had been his first role outside of comedies and rom-coms. He was sure he was going to win his supporting actor nomination. His scenes in that movie had been so intense I couldn't see how he wouldn't win. He was growing as an actor, and that film showcased his talents.

A black stretch limo picked us up from our house and drove us into downtown L.A. Memories of watching the SAG Awards from my childhood living room didn't do the experience justice.

We stepped from the limo and flashing camera lights blinded me. Sam ate up the attention, rubbing my stomach and even kissing my swollen belly. We both were on cloud nine.

I stood in awe at the celebrities who paraded down the carpet ahead of us and posed for pictures or a quick interview before going inside the venue. The spotlights added to the California heat. I was terrified I'd sweat right through my beautiful gown. The walk from the limo through the photographers and interviewers to our seats stretched out before me. I had almost begun to think we'd never make it to our seats when Sam finally guided me to our table.

Holden sat there along with two other actors that I didn't know and their dates. Energy and excitement traveled through the air of the warm room.

As the night moved along, Sam grew more anxious. He kept bouncing his knee up and down. Finally, his category was up. I drew a sharp breath as the image of me sitting with my husband splashed across the big screens set up throughout the theater.

Sam squeezed my hand and brought it to his lips, a huge grin plastered across his face as the announcer read each nominee's name. As the seconds passed, Sam's hand tightened on mine.

"And the winner is Tom Ryan!" the announcer's voice echoed across the room.

The place went wild with applause. Sam did his best to

keep his composure while the cameras were on him, but the smile melted from his face. He pressed his lips together in barely visible lines. He gave me a quick smile and joined in with the rest of the audience's applause.

He was sorely disappointed, and I was too. He had worked hard for that nomination. Still, after that initial disappointment Sam shrugged off the loss and celebrated the rest of the evening like nothing had happened.

On the ride home, Sam stared out his window in silence. I lovingly placed my hand on his and rested my head against his shoulder.

"I love you," he whispered. His voice was thick, and he almost sounded like he fought tears.

"I love you, more."

Sam wrapped his arm around me and held me the rest of the way home.

AFTER THE SHOW, Sam withdrew into himself a little. A few days later, he had a day-long meeting with a couple movie executives in Santa Monica. I decided to stay home and putter around the house. I felt huge and everything hurt.

As far along as I was things got harder and harder. Our cleaning service now came once a week, but I loathed having people in the house. I did as much for myself as I possibly could. I spent the morning cleaning and dozed off on the couch in the early afternoon. I was startled awake by the phone. I sat up and grabbed it from the side table before the answering machine clicked on.

"Mrs. Urban?" said a man.

"Yes?" I replied in confusion. No one ever called me outside of my mom and Joey.

"My name is Sergeant Martin. I'm with the Santa Monica Police Department. We have your husband in custody," he said.

"I'm sorry, what? What do you mean, 'custody?'"

"Possession of cocaine, ma'am. Now, normally, I wouldn't be calling a spouse, but I'm a big fan of your husband and he's embarrassed by this and asked me to call you and have you come down to the station to bail him out. Things like this happen, Mrs. Urban."

I wanted to reach through the phone and rip this man's throat out. Things like this didn't just happen. Even as green as I was, I knew that.

"All right, I'll be right there. Thank you." I hung up the phone and tried to force back the anxiety that threatened to turn into a full blown panic attack.

Shaking with anger and fear, I called our lawyer, then I called Holden and asked him to drive me to bail my husband out of jail. I could manage to find my way around our little area, and I could even drive parts of Rodeo Drive and Sunset Blvd. The middle of downtown L.A., where the jail was located was another story altogether. Nope, no thank you.

My emotions were all over the place. We were getting ready to have a baby, and this is what he was doing? I seethed by the time Holden got to my house.

"Did you know Sam was doing drugs?" I demanded.

Holden dropped his head. "Yes."

"How bad is it?" I asked between sobs.

Holden shifted, not wanting to meet my eyes. Finally, he sighed and ran his hand through his hair. "He's in pretty deep, Rosie. Has been for a long time. I'm surprised you didn't know."

"Well, I didn't. You supply him?"

Holden struggled for words. "We share, sometimes."

"What exactly is he on?"

When Holden finally looked up, his expression was a mixture of sympathy and sadness, causing my stomach to knot up into a hard, painful ball. I wanted to slap him.

"Whatever he can get his hands on, Rosie."

I sank down onto the couch, put my head in my hands, and sobbed.

"Oh, Rosie, honey, don't cry." Holden knelt in front of me. "Don't cry over him."

"Why didn't you tell me?" I sobbed.

Holden looked lost. "I don't.... I assumed you knew."

"Bullshit!"

"I don't know, Rosalie. Honestly, I don't. He's always been on stuff. I guess I figured it was something you would have to find out on your own. This isn't your fault, okay? This isn't something you deserve."

"Well, I'm stuck now, aren't I? I'm going to have a baby, and this is what he's doing. What the hell am I going to do?"

Holden held me as I cried. "I'm sorry," he said softly.

After a while, I stopped crying and dried my face so we could leave. Neither Holden nor I spoke on the drive.

AT THE STATION, I had to write a check for Sam's bail. I had never written one before, and I ended up having to void two before I succeeded with Holden's help. Almost an hour passed while we waited for Sam's release.

As the officers brought Sam out, he kept his eyes on the ground. My heart lurched in my chest. I closed my eyes and tried to gain my composure. I was so angry and, deep down, scared of what might come next.

Sam risked a glance at me and tried to smile. I glared, and he again dropped his gaze to the floor. I spun and walked out without a word. When he tried to take my hand in his, I snatched it away. I climbed into Holden's Jeep and slammed the door. On our way home, Sam sulked and pouted in the backseat.

"Rosalie..." he began.

"Don't! I don't want to hear your excuses, and I don't want to talk to you."

Sam narrowed his eyes but kept quiet. Holden dropped us off but didn't stay. Sam's car had been impounded, and we'd have to get it after his court hearing in the morning.

"What is wrong with you?" I asked once inside.

"Look, I get that you're pissed, okay? But this is something you wouldn't understand, so drop it," Sam said.

Sam's eyebrows knitted together, his eyes smoldering. That look told me to shut up. I lacked the ability.

"Understand? What is there to understand? I understand that my husband and the father of my unborn child is a drug addict and a liar."

"Rosalie," he warned.

"*No.* You lied to me and hid things from me. This ends now or I'm leaving."

Sam lit a cigarette with a nonchalance I knew he wasn't feeling. Head cocked, he smiled at me. In a different situation that smile would have made my heart flutter.

"You'll leave?" he said. "Take my child and leave me?"

"Absolutely," I snapped.

Sam took a long drag and nodded. Without warning, he closed the distance between us and slapped me. I stumbled back two steps. My hand flew to my face and I stared.

"Just because you're pregnant doesn't mean I won't slap the shit out of you." He grabbed a fistful of my shirt and pulled me in close. "If you ever threaten to take my child from me again, I'll kill you."

My heart pounded. Sam released me and stepped away.

"I won't raise my child around drug use." I cursed the shaky note in my voice.

"As my wife, your duty is whatever I tell you it is, and right now I'm telling you to shut up and support me." The surety and calm in his voice sent a shiver down my back.

Sam left the room to call the lawyer. I collapsed on the couch and choked back tears. I had married a monster.

Sam and I barely spoke that night. His court hearing was scheduled for first thing the next morning, and the lawyer had told Sam he would get no more than a slap on the wrist. I lay awake most of the night, struggling to sort out my feelings.

My dad was a lifelong alcoholic, so I had an idea of what addiction meant. Sam needed help. Maybe I had reacted wrongly. Maybe he really was ashamed of what happened.

I lay there remembering all the drunken fights between my parents and how, the following morning my dad would cry and beg us to forgive him. I had seen him struggle to quit drinking so many times, but something would always set him off again. Maybe that trigger was the lack of support from my mother.

Sam was right, he needed me to support him, not bitch about things. No matter what, I was going to stand behind him and be the wife he deserved. As soon as he woke up the next morning, I apologized. His face relaxed, like the weight of the world had been lifted from his shoulders.

I was just as relieved by his acceptance of my apology. This was the "for better or worse" part of my vows. I felt confident in my choice to support him rather than walk away. I knew what it felt like to need help so badly and have no one to grab on to.

Because the drug incident was Sam's first, the judge granted him drug and alcohol classes and six months of probation. He didn't even suspend Sam's driver's license. To his credit, Sam immediately started the classes, but the arrest was something we swept under the rug. How the story never made it to the media I do not know. I was only happy it didn't.

FEBRUARY BROUGHT THE ACADEMY AWARDS, and again Sam was nominated for best supporting actor, but this one was for *You Alone*, a rom-com he'd finished the week we met. He lost that one, too. After the Academy ceremony, Holden did everything he could to convince us to go to an after party.

"Come on. You guys don't have much more freedom before the baby gets here."

"Thanks anyway." Sam rubbed his hand across my huge belly. At seven months pregnant, I thought I looked like a beached whale, yet Sam insisted every day that I was beautiful. "I think we're just going to grab something to eat and go home," he said.

Holden shrugged. "Suit yourselves." He gave me a quick hug and hurried off to join the throng of party goers.

Chinese food was my biggest craving. We stopped and got take out, then went home. Sam helped me change out of my ball gown. I couldn't wait to get in an oversize t-shirt and stretchy pants. We snuggled on the couch while we ate dinner. After the movie, we cleaned up and headed upstairs to bed.

I was in the middle of some weird pregnancy dream where the baby had arrived, but I couldn't find him. Somewhere in my panicked dream mind, I vaguely heard a phone ring. Then Sam was shaking me awake.

"Rosalie, honey, wake up, please. We have to go to the hospital. Holden's in ICU."

I sat bolt upright in the bed. "What happened?"

"He overdosed. We've got to go."

WHEN WE GOT to the hospital half an hour later, reporters swarmed the entrance. We were quickly led inside by security to where Sydney, Holden's father, waited for news about Holden's condition.

"Syd, what the hell happened?" Sam demanded.

"Someone gave him a bad batch of coke. They ran some tests on the drugs found beside him and discovered opiates and heroin had been laced in the coke. They think he was down around four or five minutes, so they're hopeful that there's little to no brain damage."

Sam paled.

Sydney took a breath and started crying. "They brought him back, but he's in an induced coma to keep any swelling off his brain. The next seventy-two hours are critical. You guys can see him for a minute."

Sydney led us to Holden's room and told the nurse we were family. She gave us five minutes. Louise was sitting in a chair next to Holden lovingly stroking his hand. Her tear streaked face met mine and she gave me a small, sad smile.

"Vicky is on her way from London. I don't know how she's going to handle seeing him like this." Louise's brave mask fell as she began sobbing.

Sam immediately reached for Louise and held her. "He'll pull through this, Momma. He has to."

Louise gathered herself and patted Sam on the arm. "Talk to him. See if you can reach him."

Louise shuffled out of the room, wiping her eyes as she left. Both Sam and I gasped with emotion at the sight that greeted us. Tubes protruded from all over of Holden's body, linked to what seemed like a million beeping machines. The horrid hiss of the ventilator making his chest rise and fall was too much. Sam and I held each other and cried.

Recovering his composure, Sam took Holden's hand and leaned close. I couldn't hear what he said, but when he came up, he kissed Holden on the forehead. I kissed Holden's cheek and carefully laid my head on his chest.

"You've got to pull through this," I whispered. "You're my best friend. I can't lose you. This baby needs and deserves to know his godfather. You have to come back to us." I kissed his cheek again, then the nurse kicked us out.

As we drove home, Sam's color slowly returned. I kept stealing glances at my husband. His whole body seemed to tremble as he kept wiping at his eyes.

"Sam?" I whispered, "Are you okay?"

He barked a shaky laugh, then guided the car into an empty parking lot and parked the car.

His hands shook as he lit a cigarette. "I'm going to tell you something and please don't bitch at me. Not tonight, okay?"

I nodded and wondered what his request said about me as a wife.

"Holden.... I...." Sam broke down in sobs. After a minute, he composed himself and went on. "That should be me in the hospital."

My heart jumped into my throat. "What do you mean?"

"Holden brought some coke to the house, before the show."

"Oh my God. Did you take any?" I peered into his eyes to check his pupils but could discern nothing in the predawn light.

"No." Sam grasped my hand and kissed my palm.

"Thank you, Jesus," I breathed.

"I wanted to. More than anything, I wanted to," he said.

"But I didn't. I wanted to wait until you were asleep. Please don't be mad."

I wrapped my arms around his neck and hugged him tight. "Shh. I'm not mad. You didn't take any. That's the only thing that matters. You're safe and here in my arms and not hooked to a machine."

"I'm so sorry." Sam flicked his cigarette out of the window then turned and hugged me so tightly it hurt, but I didn't say anything.

I was so thankful he was okay, and I wanted to hold him and never let him go. A long time passed before he could collect himself enough to drive again. As soon as we got home, I followed him upstairs to our bathroom. Sam took the lid off the back of the toilet and turned it over. He removed a plastic baggie taped to the underside and dumped a grainy white powder into the water, then watched the powder swirl away with a quick flush. We stood there for a long time hugging each other. The sun was just coming up as we finally lay back down to catch some sleep.

I couldn't sleep, so I lay there and prayed, the only thing I knew to do. I prayed for Holden to recover, and I thanked God for Sam's safety. I prayed for God to give me strength, to handle this situation. I begged for Him to fix this mess and to fix Sam.

Every day of the following week, we visited Holden. As soon as Vicky's plane got in, she went straight to the hospital and stayed by Holden's side the entire time. After forty-eight hours, the doctors slowly started bringing him out of the comas. Three days later, the feeding tube came out.

Holden was extremely lucky that he came out of his overdose with only slight brain damage, mainly affecting his short-term memory. Two or three minutes longer without oxygen to his brain and he would have been much worse. After ten minutes without oxygen, the brain begins to die, and there's no coming back from that.

After two weeks in ICU, they released Holden to a drug rehab center for thirty days. Like Sam, Holden had taken any drugs he could get his hands on. He'd been that way for several years. Vicky stayed until Holden was released to the drug rehab center. Before she left, she called and invited me out to lunch. I eagerly accepted. The entire time Holden had been in the hospital she'd only spoken to Sam through glaring, blame filled eyes, so the lunch invite played slightly on my nerves.

We met at a little café on Rodeo Drive. With Holden out of the worst of things, Vicky's body language no longer held the rigid tension she'd had in the hospital. Nor did her eyes burn with the anger I'd seen directed at my husband each time we visited. Vicky waited for me just outside the café. Her face beamed as I waddled my pregnant frame over to her.

"It's so good to see you. Especially outside of the hospital." She hugged me, then pulled back and laid a hand on my belly. "Hello in there, little baby, Auntie Vicky can't wait to spoil you."

I began to relax as we went inside and the host seated us. We looked over the menu and gave our order to the waiter. The café glowed from the afternoon sun and pale, yellow walls.

"How are things? Baby growing and progressing?" Vicky asked.

"Oh, yes. I still experience morning sickness now and again, and my feet are swollen, and I sleep a lot."

"I had terrible nausea all through my pregnancy with my youngest," she said. "I definitely don't miss being pregnant."

I laughed. "I'm ready for it to be over."

Her expression turned serious. "Look, I'm sorry I was

hostile while Holden was in the ICU. I don't want you to think that was directed toward you in any way."

"No. You were fine. I can't imagine how I would be if that had been Joey."

"Every bit of that was for Sam," she said.

I blinked at her not understanding.

"Believe me there's plenty of anger toward Holden and he's only just begun hearing my mouth on the situation, but I blame Sam as much as I blame Holden," she said.

I dropped my gaze to the table. I wanted to argue that Holden was a grown man and could and had decided for himself about his drug use. I also knew that was partly bullshit because I knew Holden and Sam enabled each other. Instead of trying to speak, I shut down and stayed quiet.

"I know my brother is grown, but the truth of it is that years ago Sam is the one that introduced Holden to drugs," she said. "Holden and I aren't industry kids. We grew up in Indiana and Ohio and were older when our parents moved out here. Holden always went along with things to fit in. He made the choice to use, but Sam encourages him."

I sighed and met her gaze. "I know."

Her face softened. "I absolutely adore you, as does Holden. He told me you didn't know about Sam's drug use until recently?"

"No. I really didn't. I feel stupid now."

"Don't," she said sharply. "He's always been an expert at hiding it."

"I do believe Holden's brush with death has made Sam see the light in his own addiction," I said.

We paused our conversation as the waiter brought out our food. I prayed my strawberry crepes stayed down as they looked delicious.

When Vicky spoke again her voice trembled slightly. "For

your sake and your child's sake, I hope so, but please don't count on Sam quitting, Rosalie."

As my first bite of food slid down my throat it settled into my stomach like a ball of lead. That nagging, prickly feeling in the back of my mind hammered away.

"Holden has never truly tried to quit. I don't know whether or not he can. I'm afraid for my brother." Vicky reached across the table. Tears filled her eyes as she squeezed my hand. "Please keep an eye on him. Please help him stay clean after I go back to London. Be my eyes."

Thick emotion choked me. "Of course."

Vicky and I sat there holding hands, each of us teary eyed and looking at one another. Just as quickly as she'd drop her regal appearance and let her vulnerability shine through, Vicky cleared her throat, wiped her eyes and changed the subject to the baby that was happily letting me eat.

Despite my protests, Vicky paid the bill.

Once we were outside, she embraced me tightly. "Thank you. I believe that you are a very good influence for my brother. Here's my number." She slipped a piece of paper into my hand. "Call me just to chat and keep me updated on that darling baby. Also, don't hesitate to call if you need anything. As afraid as I am for Holden, I'm afraid for you, as well. Perhaps Holden and Sam can both prove me wrong."

We said our goodbyes and I headed home, my mind processing all that Vicky had said. I couldn't pinpoint one solid emotion, so I simply prayed for everything to work. Holden to get clean, Sam to get clean, and for everyone to just be happy and healthy.

～

Holden surprised us all and completed his rehab without incident.

Excluding Sam, he cut off all contact with anyone with whom he had previously partied. His brush with death was enough to straighten him up completely.

Sam's brush with his own mortality affected him deeply, too. He had a lot more drug paraphernalia hidden around the house than I could have possibly guesses. He had pipes, papers, and baggies of pills everywhere. I followed him from room to room as he gathered everything.

I kept my mouth shut as I watched him throw the drugs away, but inside I seethed. All of this in our house, right under my nose, and I never knew. Eventually, however, I let the anger go. He was trying, and that's what mattered. Why bitch about what was already done?

With Holden getting clean, I figured Sam would have someone who understood, someone he could lean on, giving him a better shot at getting and staying sober.

After Holden cut ties with his past, he spent a lot of time with us, telling Sam that he was living vicariously through our experiences. That was fine by me. Sam was very much the doting dad-to-be. He loved everything about my pregnancy, from the doctor appointments to the shopping to my insane food cravings at two in the morning. It wasn't uncommon for him and Holden to pile in the car in the middle of the night for a food run. I was happy to see the two most important men in my life thriving and healthy.

By the end of March, I was right at nine months, due April 2nd. Sam had landed a role in a horror movie called *Triangle* thankfully, on a local set. During my entire pregnancy, Sam only took roles in or around L.A. I was grateful he stayed so close, especially now that I was about to pop. I didn't want him to be halfway across the country when I went into labor.

Sam felt better having Holden with me while he was gone. The closer my due date got, the more nervous I became. I had zero idea what I was doing. Other than helping in the nursery at church back in Indiana, I had never been around babies. Much to Sam's displeasure, my mother decided to fly in to stay for six weeks to help me adjust.

"I don't understand why she has to be here for six weeks," he complained to Holden and me.

"Because I need her. She's my mom."

"She's a bitch," he muttered. "It's not like I can't afford a nurse or nanny."

"I don't want some stranger in our home, let alone taking care of our child, Sam."

He huffed and pouted, and I glimpsed the laugh Holden was desperately trying to hold back.

"I'm trying to stay sober, and you want me to deal with your mother for six weeks without drugs," Sam said.

"I have faith in you," I said sweetly.

Sam flipped me off.

"Besides," I said, "if you can survive my mother, you can survive anything."

"I'm only allowing this because I love you and because pregnant you is scary," he said in mock horror.

"I am not," I whined.

"Yes, you are," Holden and Sam chorused.

"Terrifying, actually." Holden grinned.

"Don't you have a home somewhere?" I snapped. Maybe I was a little bitchy.

When Mom arrived, Holden offered to pick her up, which was fine with Mom. She adored Holden, and he got along well with her. Mom being there wasn't as bad as I had anticipated. She and Sam did what they did best and pretended like the other wasn't there.

My due date came and went with no baby. Everyone treated me like a walking bomb. If I moaned over a random pain, everyone jumped like they'd heard a shot. Then it was two weeks over my due date and still no baby. I was miserable and huge, everything hurt, and I was over being pregnant. I now know the discomfort I felt that morning of the two week mark was mild contractions, but I blew them off as just back pain.

"Sometimes moving around helps," my mom said over coffee.

I rolled my eyes.

"Honestly. Sex can also help your labor start."

"I've never having sex again," I mumbled.

Mom laughed. "Why don't we go for a walk, see if that helps."

"Ugh, fine."

Sam was on the set filming just outside of downtown L.A., so Holden was in charge of driving that day. The three of us piled into his Jeep and headed for the shops on Sunset Blvd. I was swollen, hot, and miserable, but if taking a walk meant this baby would come, I'd run instead of walk.

We had just ordered from a food truck when I felt a wet, warm gush trickle down my leg.

"Oh! Uh, Mom?" I danced in place and flapped my hands in a mild panic.

"Oh, shit. Jan, what do we do?" Holden asked.

My first really hard contraction struck, and I bit my lip in an effort not to scream. My insides felt like they were being ripped apart. I grabbed at the air and finally grabbed on to Holden's hand and squeezed.

"Jan? Ow...ow...ow!" Holden cried.

"Rosalie! Breathe!" Mom barked. "Holden, we need to get her to the hospital."

"You. Have. To. Call. Sam," I hissed through sharp, stabbing pain in my abdomen.

"We will. First, we need to get going. Holden, go get the car."

"The car. Right. Rosalie, ow, ow. Rosie, you gotta let go of my hand."

Poor Holden had to pry my fingers from his hand and pass me to Mom. We'd parked the car only two blocks away, but it seemed like an eternity before Holden returned. He loaded me and Mom in the backseat, and Holden sped off toward the hospital.

He had to have broken every traffic law in Los Angeles County, and how we made it there without crashing or being pulled over I will never know. Holden was able to use the car phone to get in touch with Sam at the set, who confirmed he would meet us at the hospital.

He actually beat us there. He was waiting outside, pacing back and forth, with two nurses flanking him. Relief flooded his face when Holden brought the car to a screeching halt at the front entrance. I, on the other hand, was not as happy. I was in the worst pain I had ever experienced in my life. No amount of birthing classes had prepared me for this.

"I hate you! You did this to me, and you are never getting laid again," were my first words to my husband.

My mom patted Sam's arm. "That's normal. She doesn't mean it. You're probably going to hear a lot more before this is all over."

I sat in the wheelchair and grabbed Sam's hand. "I'm sorry."

"Shh, everything's okay," he soothed. "I know this hurts, I

love you. Ow...ow...." He grimaced when I squeezed his hand with another contraction.

Holden held his hand up. "Yeah, I think she broke mine."

"Shut up," I snapped. "Do you have something the size of a watermelon trying to come out the head of your penis? No? Then stop bitching."

The two nurses chuckled. "Today is a good day to have a baby, Mrs. Urban. Are you ready to get that little bundle of joy out?" one asked as she wheeled me inside. I nodded and breathed through another contraction.

An hour and forty-five minutes later, our son was born. Anthony Wayne Michael Urban entered the world on April 22, 1991, at 4:58 p.m. He weighed eight pounds and six ounces and was twenty-one inches long. He was a carbon copy of Sam.

I cannot remember seeing Sam happier. He actually looked younger. He was every bit the attentive father. Anthony went to the nursery only once, and that was for his recovery after being circumcised.

THE NEXT DAY, Sam granted a couple of interviews, giving *People Magazine* exclusive pictures of us in the hospital. I hated the attention. I didn't want my newborn splashed across the media, and I pointed out to Sam that those first few days were private and should stay that way.

He dismissed my protests. He was a celebrity, and therefore our life was not ours. He and Mom had a heated argument in my hospital room about the photo shoot. They got so loud that the charge nurse came in and threatened to throw everyone out, celebrity or not.

We had so many visitors that security had to be placed

outside my door. The press and paparazzi swarmed outside the hospital the following day when we went home.

I held the baby close as an orderly pushed me through the front doors out into the morning sun with Sam walking alongside. Cameras flashed and reporters shoved microphones in our faces. What should have been a sweet, private moment quickly turned into a terrifying experience when Sam got into a physical altercation with a photographer who blocked our path. The guy dropped his camera on my lap, just barely missing Anthony.

My mom had decided to stay at the house and allow Sam and I to bring Anthony home alone together. The mess with the media made me thankful she wasn't there. We were followed to our gated community, although the paparazzi were stopped at the entrance. By the time we reached home, the baby was crying, and I was in tears.

SEVEN

Sam took to being a father. All our son had to do was make the slightest noise, and Sam was at his side. Sam and my mom's relationship changed. They still didn't like each other, but they tolerated each other. They stopped taking shots at each other, which made their being in the same house easier on me.

Mom going back to Indiana was bittersweet, but I think everyone was ready for a return to normalcy. Holden spoiled Anthony as much as Sam did. There was no shortage of love in our house.

Time seemed to fly as Anthony thrived and grew. He was such an easy, happy baby. He was three months old when Sam finished his probation. I truly believed that all the bad was finally behind us. Filming for *Triangle* was wrapping up, and everything was just good. Until July 31st.

On that day, I put Anthony down for his pre-dinner nap as usual, grabbed my cigarettes along with the phone and baby monitor, and stepped out on the back porch for a smoke. I had just taken my last, blissful puff when the phone rang.

"Rosalie, listen to me and don't argue." The urgency in

Sam's voice brought me to attention. "I need you to call the lawyer and bring the checkbook down to the police station."

"What happened?"

"Just do it, please. I'll explain when you get here. Just come bail me out."

Sam hung up. No *I love you*, no nothing.

I lit another cigarette and tried to calm my nerves. What in the hell had he done now? Unsure of what to do, I called Holden.

He picked up on the second ring. "Well, hi there, pretty lady."

"Are you busy?" I asked.

"For you? Never."

"Would you be able to come get me and the baby and take me to the police station?"

"What happened?"

"I honestly have no idea," I replied. "Sam just told me to call the lawyer and get down there."

"Good Lord," he muttered. "I'm on my way."

"Thank you. I'm sorry," I said, and tried not to cry.

"Why are you sorry?"

"Every time I call you there's something wrong."

"There's nothing for you to be sorry about," he said. "Besides, this is what you do when you love someone. I'll be there soon."

We hung up, and I got the baby ready. He was extremely unhappy at being awakened from his nap and stayed fussy until Holden arrived and took Anthony into his arms.

"What's wrong with my buddy?" Holden gently rocked Anthony.

"He woke up when I changed him," I said.

In no time, Anthony quieted down I watched in amazement as he smiled at Holden. "Traitor," I muttered.

"Oh, now, Momma, he just loves his uncle," Holden baby talked at Anthony. He kissed me on the cheek. "You okay?"

"Not really. I have no idea what we're walking into."

A sad half smile touched his mouth. "You'll be okay. I'll be by your side no matter what."

THE MEDIA HAD ALREADY GOTTEN word of the arrest and were gathered outside the police station when we arrived. They descended on us like the vultures they are, shoving cameras and microphones in our faces. Holden was carrying Anthony in his car seat on one arm, trying to avoid the cameras.

We were bombarded by clicks and flashes and questions. "Mrs. Urban, can you comment on your husband's drug use? Is it true your husband was driving under the influence? Is your husband seeking help?"

A photographer burst from the crowd into Holden's way and snapped a picture of Anthony. Holden tripped and stumbled forward. I cried out as he crashed onto his side. The side of the car seat banged against the concrete, but Holden managed to right the car seat. Anthony let out an ear-screeching wail.

Holden leapt to his feet and swung at the guy. Cameras clicked and flashed, sending the crowd into a frenzy. Two police officers rushed out to help us inside. The reporter that Holden swung at screamed that he wanted to press charges.

Holden had missed the guy's nose by inches, but the asshole wanted to make something out of nothing. My nerves were frayed to the edge. I held onto Holden's arm, sobbing quietly as we pushed through the crowd. One of the cops, an older man with a thick New York accent, held up his hands to ward off the angry photographer.

"You're more than welcome to press charges," the officer told the man. "But just so you knows, you'll also be charged."

"For what? I'm the victim. He hit me."

"No, sir. You were the aggressor. I'll be charging you with child endangerment. Mr. Rae was defending the infant's safety. Yous people should all be ashamed."

The officers escorted us to a waiting room, where I was told I could speak with a detective shortly.

Holden lifted a crying Anthony from the car seat and rocked him while singing and cooing. I, on the other hand, was livid. No mother alive envisions taking their newborn to a police station to post their husband's bail.

After what seemed like hours, a detective finally joined us to explain Sam's charges. An older man with bright blue eyes, he had a gentle sense about him.

"I'm Bob Whitman. I'm sorry to have to call you down here, Mrs. Urban."

"What exactly has my husband done?" I tried to keep my voice level.

"He was observed by officers driving erratically on Rodeo Drive. When they attempted to pull him over, he tried to flee. A short-lived and slow-paced chase ensued. Your husband drove over a curb and struck a telephone pole."

"Oh my God." I rubbed the back of my hand across my forehead. I tried to make sense of what was happening. "Is he okay?"

"He's fine," the officer said. "I checked on him as soon as the patrol officers brought him in, and we've had a long conversation about what happened today. His pride is hurt more than he is. The car was towed to impound, but it isn't drivable. We aren't going to charge him with resisting."

"What are you charging him with?" Holden asked.

"Reckless driving. Possession for half an ounce of cocaine

and a handful of narcotics. He tested positive for alcohol, as well, so also a DUI."

"Jesus," I whispered. "How much is his bail?"

"Five thousand," he replied. "These are some pretty serious charges, Mrs. Urban. Luckily, no one was hurt when he struck the pole. However, this is his second drug-related arrest. I'm going to recommend that rehab be part of his sentencing. I don't believe jail is where he needs to be, but he needs help."

"Thank you."

I choked back tears. I didn't want to cry in front of this man. I didn't want his or anyone else's pity. The detective patted my hand and took us out to where I could post Sam's bail.

As the detective and I talked, Holden fed Anthony, then put the baby on his shoulder to burp him. For over an hour, I sat on the hard bench outside the booking area and let Holden hold my hand while Sam's release was being processed.

"What a fucking mess," I sighed.

Anthony, sufficiently milk drunk, slept peacefully as Holden lowered him into his car seat. "I know." He interlaced his fingers with mine. "He doesn't deserve you, Rosalie. He's never been able to hold onto his sobriety, but he's also never spiraled this far before. I'm afraid for you."

"Everything has been fine. That's what I don't understand. We haven't been fighting, and the movie is going great. I don't get it."

"You need to get away from him," Holden said.

I shook my head. "Where would I go? He'll never let me leave. You know that."

Holden opened his mouth to reply, but the door to the

booking area opened and Sam emerged into the waiting room. Holden snapped his mouth shut.

"Let's get out of here, please," Sam said under his breath.

Holden buckled Anthony's into the car seat, then straightened. Sam reached for the car seat handle, but Holden smacked his hand away.

"No," Holden snapped.

"No?" Sam's eyes narrowed. "What the hell, Holden? He's my kid."

"You're still coming down from coke and pills. I can see it in your eyes, and you're sweating like a pig. You are not carrying him."

They glared at each other and, for a moment, I thought they would start swinging. To my relief, the same officer who helped us get inside the station came out to escort us to our car. The press outside had turned into chaos.

Sam grabbed my hand. I tried pulling free, only to have my hand crushed. The last thing I wanted was for him to touch me, so I tugged harder in an effort to pull free. Sam's hold tightened painfully and I gave up. I had to let him hold my hand, or he would break it.

Holden's car seemed so far away in the midst of the blinding camera flashes. Dozens of reporters followed, screaming all kinds of vulgar questions. "Do you think your drug use is becoming a problem?"

"How do you feel about the father of your child being on drugs, Mrs. Urban?"

I ignored them and kept my eyes down. We reached the car and I purposely took the front passenger seat while Holden strapped Anthony in the back with Sam. Once inside the car, Holden locked the doors. No one said a word as he started the engine and pulled away. Reporters pounded on the hood and Holden shouted that he would run them over if they didn't get out of the way.

"Is there even a point to my apologizing?" Sam asked after a few minutes.

"No," Holden and I said in unison.

"Okay. I get why you're pissed, Rosalie. But what the hell is your problem, Holden?"

Holden chuckled deep in his chest, but he was anything but amused. The sound remined me of a thunderstorm rumbling in the distance.

I swallowed. *Oh shit.*

"This stuff almost killed me, and you're willing to risk your life for a fix?" Holden snapped. "You have an amazing wife who stands beside you no matter what. You have a beautiful, healthy son, and you're willing to throw all that away. Why?"

"Because he's stupid," I muttered.

"What? What did you say?" Sam roared. Suddenly, he leaned forward and smacked me across my face.

Holden slammed on the brakes and yanked the car to the side of the road. Behind us, horns blared as we shuddered to a stop. Holden threw off his seat belt and spun to face Sam. He reached back and slapped Sam across his face.

The sharp crack was deafening in the confined space. For a moment the Jeep remained deathly silent, then Holden's anger roared to life.

"How do you like being hit?" he hissed. "Hit her again, and I'll kill you!"

Sam cowered against the back seat. Holden faced forward, refastened his seat belt, then carefully pulled back into traffic. In a tense silence, we drove home, where Holden carried Anthony inside.

He gave Anthony a gentle kiss on the cheek, then hugged

me. "You need anything at all, you call me, no matter what time."

I nodded.

"Holden," Sam began.

"Shut up, Sam," he said through clenched teeth. "You are unbelievable. We've been friends since we were little kids. I refuse to watch you kill yourself over this stuff. Get your shit together."

Holden stalked from the living room and slammed the front door behind him. I took Anthony from his car seat and put him in his playpen with a few toys.

"What in the hell were you thinking?" I demanded. I didn't care if I made him mad.

"Don't start."

"Ha! You bet your ass I'm going to start."

"Just shut up. This isn't something you would understand. Let it go," he growled.

"That's your solution to everything. Ignore the problem and it'll go away. This isn't going away. You endangered not only yourself but innocent people as well. Not to mention, your arrest will be splashed across every magazine and newspaper across the country. How stupid are you?"

Sam strode to me. "Shut up, Rosalie. I'm only going to warn you once."

I was too angry to care. "Or what, Sam? You'll hit me? Go for it!"

He drew back his hand, and I flinched. I waited, tensed for the blow, but his hand remained frozen midair.

"Damn it, Rosalie." Sam fisted his hand. He shook with rage. At last, he turned and went upstairs.

I released the breath I didn't know I was holding. Shaking, I changed Anthony and played with him for a few minutes. I was so angry and numb that I returned him to the playpen so I could go outside to smoke. Dozens of thoughts flew through my head, and I couldn't focus.

Eventually, I calmed down enough to start dinner. When the food was prepared, I went upstairs to let Sam know dinner was served. He wasn't in our bedroom, so I went to his office and pushed open the door. Sam leaned over this desk, snorting one of five straight, fine lines of white powder.

"What in the hell are you doing?" I cried. "Are you kidding me?"

He whirled to face me. "Rosalie...I...."

"Don't bother." I stormed to the desk and swept my hand across the top, sending the powder flying into the air and onto the floor.

"You bitch!"

"You're sick. Our child is downstairs, and you're snorting drugs?"

I grabbed the baggie with the remaining powder and ran for the bathroom. I slammed the door but got the lock only halfway latched. Sam screamed and pounded as I tried with shaking hands to open the bag. Suddenly Sam slammed into the door. The wood splintering and the door flung open and hit the wall with a loud crack.

"What do you think you're doing?" he yelled.

I managed to get the bag open and dumped the powder in the toilet. With an animal growl, Sam leapt for me and pinned me to the floor. He hit my face, shoulders and arms.

"You stupid bitch," he bellowed. "You just cost me two grand."

I shoved as hard as I could and managed to push him away. I scrambled to my feet and stumbled into the bedroom. He grabbed my hair and yanked me backwards. My scalp felt like it was on fire. I screamed. He grabbed my right hand and twisted. There was no mistaking the sharp snap. White hot pain dropped me to my knees. I scooted across the carpet and collapsed against the wall, cradling my hand.

"Jesus wept, Sam! You broke my wrist."

"You should have learned your place by now," he snarled. "I'm sorry, Rosalie." The glassy look in his eyes had disappeared, now replaced with guilt as his face reddened.

I stared, my eyes wet with tears. "Do you even know the meaning of that words?"

"You forced me to do this." He continued to look anywhere but my eyes.

"I forced you to beat me?"

Sam's head jerked up. That hollow, empty look had returned. "I haven't beaten you. Not yet, anyway."

"You touch me again and I swear to God I'll—"

Sam took two quick steps to me, then seized my shirt front and pulled me to my feet. "You'll what, Rosalie? Don't ever think of threatening me. I warned you once. The only way you are ever leaving me is in a body bag."

He shoved me, and I stumbled, catching myself against the wall with my injured wrist. I groaned in pain.

Sam laughed. "You should get that looked at. I know, call your boyfriend. I'm sure he'll rush right over to be at your side. Whore."

Anthony began to cry. Sam and I looked in the direction of the door, then he whirled and strode from the room. I followed, hard on Sam's heels as he descended the stairs. He was higher than a kite, and I was afraid he'd try to take Anthony. But he walked right past his son, grabbed his keys from the coffee table, and left.

I shushed Anthony softly. Pain shot through my throbbing wrist, but I gritted my teeth and tried to use my arm with the wounded wrist. I had a heart-stopping moment when I thought I would drop him, but I managed to get him out of the playpen. I didn't want to call Holden, but I couldn't care for Anthony with a broken wrist. I couldn't even get him in his car seat.

I sat on the couch and tried to calm my racing emotions. Anthony fussed and I knew he could sense my stress. This was it. I was stuck in a nightmare marriage. As much as I loved Sam, he was never going to let me go. With a shaky hand, I picked up the phone from its base on the side table and dialed Holden's number.

"How bad this time?" he answered.

My heart skipped a beat with the memory of the crack when Sam twisted my hand. "My wrist is broken," I whispered.

"Jesus." He blew out a breath. "Sit tight. I'm on my way." His keys jingled in the background.

I rocked Anthony as I waited. Sam needed help, and all I was doing was making it worse for him. If I just hadn't freaked out, he wouldn't have beaten me. Holden arrived in record time. When he burst through the front door, I was kicking myself about the whole incident.

"Let me see." Holden examined my hand.

I flinched when he touched my wrist.

His brow furrowed. "Sorry, honey. Yeah, that's broken all right."

"Holden, I'm sorry."

"This isn't your fault."

"I'm ruining your friendship with Sam."

Holden took Anthony from me and rocked him. "What in the hell would make you say that?"

"You were his friend first. You have no responsibility to me."

"He may be my friend, but that doesn't mean what he's doing is right."

"I feel like shit," I said. "Something happens, I call you, and you come rushing over here like my knight in shining armor."

Holden was tickling Anthony and pretending to eat his fingers. "Is that what I am?"

I gave a shaky laugh. "My hero."

Holden squeezed my good hand. "I'll take that. Please don't feel bad. I told you to call me."

"You must be tired of rescuing me."

"I'm tired of you getting hurt, but I'm not tired of being there for you," he said. "This is what you do for someone you love."

EIGHT

INSTEAD OF THE ER we went to an urgent care facility on the outskirts of Los Angeles County. The receptionist along with the two nurses standing in the front area recognized Holden and I immediately. They fell all over Holden—and cooed over Anthony. To be fair, Holden didn't have to do much of anything to have the ladies swoon over him.

Very slowly I took my sunglasses off. The receptionist's sharp intake of breath told me she knew.

"Look, you obviously know who I am," I said. "I need this visit kept quiet, please." With my undamaged hand I pulled a wad of cash from my pocket and sat it on the counter.

I watched the situation I had just put this young lady in war behind her eyes. The older of the two nurses stepped over and I repeated my request. For several heart stopping moments, the receptionist just looked at me. I could feel the tears threatening to break free of my resolve. Finally, she took the cash and nodded.

I followed her to an examination room and waited inside while she went to speak with the doctor. The doctor that finally entered the exam room was in his sixties with snow white hair. The nurse stood in the corner, silent.

"I see here you've had quite a fall, ma'am," he said.

I nodded.

"You know, most situations that lead to these kinds of falls don't get better." He looked at me through his narrowed eyes ad held contact for so long that I had to look away. "Don't you worry, though. We'll get you fixed up. But I might suggest that you avoid and get away from whatever tripped you up today."

They put my wrist in a cast and sent me home. As I gathered my purse the nurse handed me a pamphlet before patting my good arm and leading me back out into the waiting room.

Once we got outside, I looked at the pamphlet. It was from CODA and gave a list of resources for domestic violence. I wadded the paper and dropped it on the ground and suppressed a shudder. I didn't want to think about what Sam would do if he found something like that in my purse. Holden held my good hand all the way back. I was so numb I couldn't even cry.

When we turned into the driveway, my heart sped up. Sam's car sat in the driveway. Without a word, Holden shut the car off and helped me out, then got Anthony, who slept in his car seat. Sam rose from the couch as we entered. His gaze locked on my cast and tears filled his eyes.

"I'm sorry, Rosalie," he whispered.

Holden sat Anthony's car seat on the far side of the room, then calmly walked over to Sam, and decked him in the mouth.

"Holden! Don't!" I shrieked, as Sam's head snapped back.

He stumbled backward, then caught himself. He locked eyes with Holden an rubbed his jaw. "I deserve that." A smug smile curved Sam's lips.

"That and so much more." Holden drew back his hand again.

"Holden, please don't," I begged.

Holden glared at Sam for a long moment, then lowered his arm. "You've got the whole world right in front of you, Sam, and you're going to end up killing her. Don't touch her again."

Holden took three steps to me, kissed me on the forehead, then left us alone. Neither Sam nor I spoke. I got Anthony unbuckled and out of his seat, then carried him upstairs to change him and put him to bed. As he settled into a quiet sleep in his crib, I stroked his head.

"How bad's the break?"

I whirled. Sam stood in the doorway, his arms crossed. With some satisfaction, I noticed the bruising that had begun to form on his cheek.

"I'll be in the cast for a few weeks." I turned and busied myself folding a small basket of Anthony's clothes that had been forgotten in the turmoil of the day.

Sam crossed the room to stand behind me. He put his hands on my shoulders and began rubbing them. I tensed even as I tried not to. I didn't want to anger him any more than I already had.

"I'm sorry, Rosalie...about everything. There is no excuse, but when you took the drugs, I just snapped. I'm sorry."

Hugging me from behind, he laid his head on my shoulder. I could feel his tears on the back of my neck.

"I need help, Rosalie. I'm sorry. I didn't really mean to hurt you." His voice broke, and he sobbed.

I turned and threw my arms around him. "I'm sorry I made things worse."

"Let's go to bed," he said.

We went to the bedroom and made love, slow and gentle,

reminding me of our first time. We fell asleep holding each other.

Court was at nine the next morning. The judge ordered Sam to pay for the damage to the pole and suspended his license for six months. He also ordered Sam into a rehab facility for thirty days followed by six months formal probation. Sam had until Monday to turn himself in.

Our lawyer had already taken care of the facility arrangements. We went straight to the rehab facility from the courthouse so we could get a tour and an overview of Sam's stay.

My stomach remained in knots all day. Thirty days really isn't that long, but to me it seemed an eternity. From day one, I hadn't been away from Sam for more than his workday hours. Such a lengthy stay seemed like an eternity.

We spent the weekend doing as many things as we could together. We made each moment together count, whether watching TV, cooking, or cleaning. Sam took over completely with Anthony and refused to let me help. He and Holden even made up, at least on Sam's end. I knew Holden wasn't the least bit sorry for punching Sam, no matter what he said.

On Monday, Sam asked Holden to drive us to the facility because I did not trust myself to drive back. I was a complete mess. Neither of us had slept the night before. I did nothing but cry. I was making it worse, but I couldn't stop myself.

Sam put on a brave front, but when we pulled into the facility, he finally let loose and cried. He kissed Anthony on the head and stroked his tiny hand. "Daddy loves you." Sam clung to me. "I'm so sorry about this."

"It's okay," I murmured. "This is going to help us in the long run."

Reluctantly, Sam finally released me. "Please take care of them," he said to Holden.

"Always have," he answered.

Long after Sam disappeared inside the building, Holden and I stood there as I cried and cried. My heart was being ripped out. Finally, I got myself together, and we went home. Holden offered to stay, but I told him no.

"I just really need some time to process what has happened," I told him.

He nodded. "I understand. Promise you'll call me if you need anything?"

"I promise."

He gave Anthony and I a kiss and left. The house felt so empty and strange without Sam. I probably cried a hundred times that day.

THE BETTER PART of a week passed before I got into a routine. Holden visited every day and, more often than not, we went out to eat or to shop. Sometimes we took Anthony to the park and sometimes we took him to Holden's parents' house in Malibu. They adored Anthony like he was their own grandchild.

The media had a field day with Sam being in rehab, publishing picture after picture of Holden and me together along with bullshit rumors about us. One had us on the cover walking down Sunset Boulevard together: *Is Holden Rae moving in on best pal Sam Urban's child bride?*

The invasion into my private life was disgusting. I didn't understand how these magazines could write such hateful and untrue stories.

Finally, at the end of August, Sam came home. I was so happy. I bought ingredients to make every one of his favorite meals. When I arrived at the rehab facility with Anthony to pick Sam up, a small crowd of paparazzi waited in front of the building. Nothing was ever private.

"Fucking vultures," Sam said, climbing into the car.

"It's been a nightmare. I can't go anywhere or do anything without them following me," I said.

"I know. I didn't think my problems would bring this much attention."

"They've got to be breaking some law," I grumbled.

"As long as they're on a public street, we're fair game, honey."

"They make up disgusting lies to sell stories."

"No one said they were ethical, babe."

"That's for sure," I growled. "Trusted sources" and "sources close to the star" rarely exist. Those statements are nothing more than a way to make a writer's opinions seem true.

For all of our legal troubles, Sam had no shortage of work. During the next three months, he landed several guest spots on television, mostly dramas and a couple of comedies, which minimized his time away from home.

His six months of probation included random drug tests, and Sam seemed to be passing them all. Life began blissful. In the first four months, we rarely fought, and not once did he hit me. I hosted our first anniversary and second Thanksgiving together as one big holiday party. Sam even flew my parents in for the holiday.

I made a big to-do with the food. Thanksgiving had always been my favorite holiday. Preparing and hosting Thanksgiving was one of the rare things my mother and I did together when I was growing up. Thanksgiving and Christmas were the only times in my childhood that held good memories. The only time we didn't fight.

The downside to this Thanksgiving was that Sam's parents were also coming. When it came to Cassandra, Sam's mother, nothing I did was good enough, and she insisted on calling Anthony "Tony". She made such a fuss over Anthony that she sent him into a bout of tears. They had only seen him once, right after he was born, and hadn't made another effort to bond with him since.

With my parents, Sam's parents, Joey, Holden, and Holden's parents, we had a full house. Of course, Cassandra pushed me until I hit my breaking point in front of everyone.

I gathered everyone in the living room for appetizers while my turkey finished browning. My mom kept eyeing Cassandra and rolling her eyes every time the woman spoke. Biting my lip to keep from giggling I passed a tray of stuffed mushrooms around.

"What size clothes is little *Tony* in now?" Cassandra asked.

I gritted my teeth. "Cassandra, for the last time, his name is Anthony, not Tony."

"Oh, please dear, all grandparents have little nicknames for their grandchildren."

"Goddamn it," Sam muttered. He already knew what was coming.

I pinned Cassandra with a glare. "Oh? You're a grandmother now? When I was pregnant you said you were too young to be one."

"I meant I was too young to be called Grandma, dear."

"Well, when he can call you "Grandma" in front of everyone, you can call him Tony," I said smugly.

"Sammy, aren't you going to say something?" his mother demanded.

Sam put his arm around my waist. "No, Mom. He's our son, and you need to respect our wishes."

My mom just beamed at Sam while Cassandra huffed and puffed. Plopping down on my couch, she crossed her arms and stuck out her bottom lip. I couldn't believe that a grown woman literally pouted like a child. After a few minutes, she retrieved a gold cigarette case from her purse and lit one.

"You can't smoke in here," I said.

"Why not? You both smoke."

"We smoke outside, Mom," Sam said.

His eyes pleaded with me to not make this a thing. I ignored him. I was making this a thing.

"You cannot smoke around my son," I said.

"This is my son's house," she shot back.

"Your son may have paid for this house, but I run it. You are welcome to smoke outside."

Everyone stared at us, like they didn't know whether to laugh or leave. Cassandra rose and marched to the backyard, muttering the whole way. I returned to the kitchen to finish cooking. Holden followed and gave me a side hug.

"That's my girl," he whispered.

Out of the corner of my eye, I noticed Sam watching from the doorway. He didn't look happy, but I didn't care. The rest of the evening went off without any more problems. My parents were staying for the weekend and having them and Sam under the same roof kept me on edge. At least they were being civil for Anthony's sake.

After everyone either left or retired for the night, Sam and I went upstairs. He was leaving the next morning to film his guest spot on *Streets*, a TV crime drama. Filming was in Santa Barbara, which was two hours away, with a shooting schedule of twelve to fourteen hours a day, Sam thought staying the weekend at a hotel would be easier than driving back home each day.

While he was gone, I planned on taking my mother to the Black Friday sales, and I looked forward to enjoying some time with her. I didn't even realize Sam was in a mood until he spoke.

"So, what did your boyfriend have to say in the kitchen earlier?"

I had no idea what he was talking about. I just looked at him like he was stupid.

"Earlier, you and Holden in the kitchen?" he said. "After the ordeal with my mom?"

"He just said good for me for standing up for myself," I replied. "Why in the hell are you calling him my boyfriend?"

"You two have gotten awfully chummy."

I rolled my eyes. "Are you kidding?"

"I'm just stating the obvious."

"Sam, you've lost your mind. I love you. Holden is the only friend I have here. Don't take that from me, please."

"You love me, huh?"

"Yes." I braced for the fight I thought was coming, but Sam surprised me and pulled me to him. He kissed me like he had our first night together.

"Show me," he whispered.

We made love twice that night. It would be the last time for three months.

We rose before dawn, and I made everyone breakfast. After sending Sam off for the weekend with a kiss, I left with Mom while Dad stayed home with Anthony. I thought Black Friday sales back home in Indiana were bad, but nothing had prepared me for Los Angeles. I treated my mom to high-end stores that she'd never been able to afford, putting the limited choices back in Terre Haute to shame.

The experience was fun and draining and full of mystery. These high society women didn't play when it came to their sales. We weren't in any real danger, but the shoppers were aggressive, pushing and shoving their way in like I had never seen.

After I treated my parents to dinner that night, we went home, where I talked to Sam on the phone before going to bed. I drifted off to sleep, feeling very loved and very lucky.

Around four a.m. the following morning, the phone woke me. Detective Whitman, the same detective from Sam's second arrest, told me Sam had been arrested again. Several groggy minutes passed before I fully understood the situation.

"I don't get this. Sam's supposed to be in Santa Barbara," I said.

"He was picked up in downtown L.A., Mrs. Urban."

I swung my legs over the edge of the bed. I was so tired of this. "How much is bail?"

"No bail this time," he replied.

"I don't understand."

"Mrs. Urban...."

"Rosalie, please," I said.

"Rosalie, your husband is on probation, so when he was brought in, we notified his probation officer. Mr. Urban tested positive for cocaine, I'm afraid."

A million thoughts raced through my mind, but I needed to focus on this moment. "What are the other charges?"

"Public intoxication, possession of an illegal substance, violation of probation."

"So, what happens now?" I asked, trying to remain calm.

"He'll sit in county until his court appearance Monday morning."

"Great."

"Rosalie, I am very sorry about this. I really believe he needs help. I've seen a lot of addicts come and go, seen a lot of celebrities, too, but I believe your husband can overcome this."

"He has to want to first," I said.

"I know. I normally don't bend the rules for anyone, but if

you can get down here, I'd be willing to let you see him for a few minutes."

"I'll be right there. Thank you so much."

I hung up and quickly got dressed. I was too angry to think. I knew what pot smelled like. As a teenager, Joey had gone through a year-long pot phase before Dad kicked him out. I would never forget that smell, so unless Sam had been going outside, I knew pot wasn't in his arsenal of habits.

I hadn't seen signs of any other drugs, but obviously I hadn't been paying close enough attention. I didn't have time to search the house now, but I would when I got back and so help me God if I did find drugs, I'd flush them all.

Once I was ready to go, I woke my mom.

"What's wrong? Is the baby okay?" she asked sleepily.

"Anthony's fine. He's asleep, but I need you to watch him for a while."

"What's going on?"

I fought back tears. "Sam's been arrested, again. I do not have time to go into this right now. I just need you to watch Anthony."

She sat up. "Go. I've got him."

I hurried downstairs to the car. I was trying to be a good wife and support Sam. I was trying not to be a hateful, nagging wife, but Sam's drug problem had become too much.

I replayed the entire weekend in my mind. Why was Sam in Los Angeles when he was supposed to be in Santa Barbra? What other lies were there between us, besides the drug use? An affair? I I refused to consider the idea and shut that thought-train down quickly.

Sam's arrest must have been quick and quiet because there was no press when I arrived at the police station. Detective Whitman was waiting for me at the desk.

Giving me a sad smile, he shook my hand. "I'm sorry we keep meeting like this."

"So am I."

"I can give you about fifteen minutes with him."

"I don't know why you're doing this for me but thank you."

He escorted me to an interrogation room, where Sam waited inside.

"Thank you," Sam said quietly.

"You're welcome." Detective Whitman closed the door, leaving me alone with my husband.

NINE

Sam hunched, his wrists shackled and secured to the table where he sat. His face was red, and his teary, swollen eyes met mine. My anger waned. Seeing my husband in handcuffs tugged at my heart, even if this wasn't the first time.

"What in the hell are you doing, Sam?" I demanded in a low, thick whisper.

"I don't know anymore."

"You're supposed to be in Santa Barbara. How did you end up in LA and arrested?"

"I'm sorry," he said, his voice cracking.

I shook my head. "I don't want to hear that. Answer my question."

Sam dropped his gaze. "Me and some of the guys went clubbing and decided to come to LA."

I knew there was more to it than that. "Did you get the drugs there or here?"

"Here," he mumbled.

"Oh, so you came home to get the drugs?"

Silence. Which I took as a yes.

"I am trying to be a good, supportive wife, but you're not giving me anything to work with," I said,

He yanked his head up and shouted, "This is not easy for me, Rosalie."

"No?" I rolled my eyes. "You have an almost unlimited income, you're an A-list star, and we own a beautiful home. You have a wife who worships you and a healthy, beautiful son. Please tell me how you have it so bad."

"You wouldn't understand."

"What is there to understand? My husband is a drug addict."

Sam scowled. "Are you or Anthony going hungry? Are you working two jobs to keep the utilities on? Are we on welfare? No? Then don't fucking call me an addict."

"You're throwing everything away," I retorted.

"You are not going anywhere. You understand that, right?" he said in a quiet voice.

"I didn't say I was."

"Not in so many words. But your mother is here, and I can only imagine what she's already put in your head. I just don't want you getting any ideas."

I glared. "I hadn't planned on going anywhere."

"Well, should you have any ideas, keep in mind that when I get out, I will find you. I will drag you back here, even if that means you're not breathing."

The words had been spoken low and even. My heart thudded in my ears. The room began to spin. Threats came so easily to him.

"Besides," he shrugged, "if you do leave me, I'll make sure you lose custody of Anthony."

I couldn't believe what he'd just said. I stared.

"Money talks, honey," he went on in a cordial tone. "If you

leave, you don't have the means to take care of our son like I do."

He had me there. I sank onto the chair across from Sam. I dropped my head into my hands. I wanted to cry, but nothing came. I desperately tried to slow my pounding heart, afraid that I might pass out. Sam touched my hand. I snapped my head up.

"Look, I'm sorry," he said. "I messed up. What more do you want me to say?"

"I want this to stop. I want you to stop, Sam."

"I'm trying. I know you don't believe that, but I am. I can't get away from the drugs."

"You have to, Sam."

"I know."

"Do you love me?" I asked.

His eyes widened. "Of course, I do."

"Then why can't that be enough for you to stop?"

"I don't want to lose you, Rosalie. The drugs are like drowning, and I like the feeling of water in my lungs."

I shook my head. I couldn't understand that. But I did understand that his addiction was the only thing that mattered to him. As far as Sam was concerned, he was in control. I didn't know at what made him believe that. Maybe because he didn't fit the stereotypical drug user, at least in his mind, his using wasn't a problem. I now understood that his addiction controlled him, not the other way around.

"Do you still love me?" Sam asked.

It was my turn to be startled. I didn't think he gave a damn what I thought. Couldn't he tell? Hadn't I stayed devoted to him despite everything?

"Of course I do. How can you possibly ask me that?"

He shrugged. "All the shit I've put you through. I know that my actions don't match my words, but I do love you."

Tears pricked my eyes. "I know you do."

"I'm sorry, honey." Sam's tears flowed as easily as mine.

"Help me, Sam. Help me save us."

We held each other and cried until the detective returned. It was time for me to go.

"I'll call you later this afternoon," Sam said.

I faked a smile. I wanted things to work, I wanted him to get help and fix our marriage. I didn't want him to see how sad and scared I truly was.

"I love you, Rosalie."

"I love you, too." I gave Sam a kiss, then followed the detective out.

I DIDN'T WANT to go back home and face my mother. If Anthony hadn't been with her, I probably wouldn't have. But I did return home. I found her sitting at the kitchen table, a pot of fresh coffee waiting.

"Baby's still sleeping," she said.

I slumped into a chair and fished around in my purse for my cigarettes.

"I thought we couldn't smoke in here," she teased as I lit one.

"My rules, I can break them." I opened the patio door, then hunted for an ashtray while Mom lit herself a cigarette. Unable to find an ashtray, I grabbed a saucer from the cabinet.

I chuckled as I sat it down on the table. "God, Sam would kill me if he saw me use a saucer."

My mom looked at me funny. Her eyes searched mine as I desperately tried to push her intrusive stare away.

Ah, shit.

"Is he hitting you?" she asked.

"Of course not," I scoffed. "Just a turn of phrase."

My stared and I fought the urge to squirm under her gaze. "Rosalie...."

"Mom, he's not hitting me. Stop," I warned.

The silence between us seemed to stretch into eternity.

"What happened?" she finally asked.

I sighed. "He got caught with drugs, again. Cocaine, this time. There is no bail since it's a probation violation. We have court first thing Monday morning."

She shook her head. "Jesus Christ. You're going to stay with him?"

I was so not in the mood for this conversation. "Of course I am. I'm his wife."

"What a great example the two of you are setting for my grandson," she spat.

"Like the example you and Dad gave me?"

She gave me a death stare and flicked her ash before speaking. "I was hoping you would learn from my mistakes. This man doesn't love you or Anthony. When are you going to see that? If he did, he wouldn't be getting arrested."

I gritted my teeth. "I am learning from *your* mistakes, Mother. I am standing beside my husband by actually trying to help him get and stay sober."

"Rosalie, you may think you're now a woman of the world, but you don't know a damn thing. That boy is hell bent on destruction, and he's going to take you with him."

"Just let me handle my marriage, okay?" I snapped. "I don't need your input."

I was saved from further discussion by my son's cries. I went upstairs to change him and brought him downstairs to start the day. Why did everything have to be such mess? This wasn't how my life was supposed to be.

. . .

SAM'S ARREST made the morning news. The phone rang shortly after the broadcast. Mom sat with Anthony on the couch and she glanced up. I ignored her and scooped up the phone from the living room coffee table and answered.

"How are you holding up?" Holden asked.

"I don't even know anymore," I replied.

"Do you need anything?"

"Yeah, my husband to choose me over damn drugs." I burst into tears.

Holden listened to me grieve for someone who wasn't dead. Finally, I gathered myself together.

"Sorry," I said.

"That's what I'm here for. How long are your parents staying?" he asked.

"Dad is leaving Sunday, and Mom is staying until Monday afternoon, so I don't have to take Anthony to court with me."

"Come out with me tonight, take your mind off everything."

I hesitated. "I don't think that's a good idea, Holden."

"What idea?" Mom asked.

I knew she had been pretending not to be interested in the conversation by the way she busied herself with dusting.

"Come on, Rosie. Get out of the house for a while and have some fun," Holden said. "Let your mom enjoy her time with the baby."

"Yeah, but how will that look?" I asked.

"Who gives a shit? You need out of the mindset you're in."

"Sam's in jail. I can't go out for fun."

"Rosalie, seriously, you need some time to yourself," he insisted.

"I'll think about it."

Holden sighed. "Well, that's as close to a yes as I'm gonna get. I'll call you this evening."

"All right," I laughed, and hung up.

Would it really be so terrible if I went?

Of course. What in the hell was I thinking? Sam was sitting in jail, and I was contemplating a night out. I definitely wasn't going.

The phone rang again an hour later. This time it was Joey. I let Mom talk to him and explain about Sam. Joey had begun a new relationship with a wonderful guy named Paul, and the last thing I wanted to do was mess with his happiness. I also didn't want my older brother guessing just how bad things really were between Sam and me.

Sam called after lunch. He had sobered up, so it was an emotional conversation full of *I love you's* and *I'm sorry's*. I asked Sam what he thought about Holden's idea.

"Holden's right," he said. "You need to get out of the house and away from things for a bit. Besides, you're safe with Holden, and I know he won't try anything."

Okay. So, I was going?

"I don't feel right," I told my mom after I hung up.

"You're going out with a friend. Your husband knows and approves. What is there to feel bad about?"

"My husband is in jail. He can't be here. He can't go out and get his mind off things."

"He made his bed, now he has to lie in it," she replied in a kinder voice than expected. "Just because he's in jail doesn't mean you are."

But she didn't understand. I *was* in jail with Sam. Not physically, but I was right there with him. Arguing was a waste of time, so I kept the thought to myself.

I DRESSED in a simple black dress and low heels since I didn't know where Holden planned on going. Knowing Holden, it would be subtle, which is what I craved. Some sense of normal.

He arrived close to seven in a simple dark blue suit.

"Beautiful as always." He gave me a quick hug. "Are you sure you don't mind, Jan?" he asked my mother.

"Not at all. She needs a night away," Mom assured him.

"We might be back late," Holden said. I gave him a puzzled look and he added, "You need a night out of LA and away from cameras and people. I thought we'd go to Long Beach."

"I think that's a wonderful idea," Mom said before I could protest.

Holden winged an arm. "Ready?"

I kissed Anthony on the cheek then slipped my arm through Holden's and we left.

Holden chatted lightly about his upcoming movie and a few projects he was considering. I didn't say much.

"It's okay to talk, you know. It's just me, Rosie," he said.

I smiled. "I know, I just feel weird. Sam is in jail, and I'm going out on the town."

"No, you're out with a friend, taking a break and recharging. You cannot take care of Sam and Anthony if you're run down."

I guess that made sense. I wasn't going behind Sam's back. And this was Holden, for God's sake.

"You're right." I relaxed a little.

"There's my beautiful girl."

"How do you do it, Holden? How do you stay sober?"

"Almost dying helped," he said with a mirthless laugh. "I never want to go through that again. I got lucky. Besides, I have a best friend and a beautiful godson. I never again want to risk losing the people I love."

I burst into tears. Holden pulled to the side of the road and wrapped his arms around me. "Oh, honey, please don't cry."

"Why can't I be enough for Sam?" I blubbered. "Am I that awful that he has to do this?"

"Listen to me, there's nothing wrong with you. Sam does drugs and gets high because he can, because he's fucking stupid. He has no idea what he has in front of him."

"I don't know how to make him see that, either," I sniffed.

"You can't, honey. He has to want to, and right now he can't see past his addiction."

Eventually I stopped crying. I pulled a tissue from my purse and cleaned myself up in the mirror.

"Feel better?" Holden asked.

I nodded. I did, a little.

"New rule for tonight." Holden started the car. "No more tears. Tonight, there are no problems, no husbands in jail, no sadness. Deal?"

No promises, I thought, but said, "Deal."

HOLDEN TOOK me to a cozy restaurant with a dance floor. I love to dance. We started with drinks at the bar and danced a few songs while we waited for a table. I was surprised to realize I was having fun.

"You got some moves, little girl," Holden said. He was out of breath and grinning.

"Thank you, thank you." I sipped my wine.

The waiter interrupted to let us know our table was ready. Holden held my seat for me, then took the chair opposite me. He gazed at me. Butterflies fluttered to life in my stomach. Love shone so brightly in his eyes that I wanted to lose myself in them. But I couldn't.

"What?" I laughed.

"Do you realize how beautiful you are?"

"Holden..." My face grew hot.

"No. You are," he said. "You look happy."

"Well, I have you to thank for that," I said.

Holden leaned forward and caressed my face. If swooning was a real thing, I would've fallen right out of my chair. I took a deep breath to steady my pounding heart. We ordered dinner and chattered like best friends who hadn't seen each other in forever. We shared a deep love of all things dark and morbid, like horror movies, scary books, and anything paranormal. We talked about our favorite books and movies, and I was surprised to find that Holden was an avid reader like me.

Our conversation jumped all over the place. We could start on one topic, then go off on two or three different ones, and come back like we'd never gotten off track.

For the first time in a while, I felt good...normal. We had just finished dessert when Holden's favorite song, "Angel Eyes" by The Jeff Healy Band, began to play.

"You have to dance with me, Rosalie." He stood and extended a hand.

Holden held me tight while humming along to the song. I lost myself in the words and his embrace. As the song ended, he gave me a twirl and then bowed. The room filled with applause. Holden hugged me to him, laughing.

"Did you enjoy yourself?" he asked as we walked back to the table.

"Yes, I absolutely did. Thank you."

We enjoyed a couple more songs. A few people recognized Holden and asked for his autograph, which he happily gave before we left.

In my driveway, neither of us was in a hurry to get out of the car.

"I wish I could make Sam see things from my point of view. I'd give anything to change things for you, Rosalie," Holden said.

"That's sweet. I appreciate the thought."

"I'm glad I could make you happy tonight," he said softly.

"You did. Thank you. You were right, I really did need this."

"I'm glad to be of service." He hugged me.

Holden hugging me or even giving me a kiss on the cheek or forehead was nothing new, even in front of Sam. But this time was different. He lingered, his face close enough that his warm breath bathed my neck. He pulled back so that his mouth hovered above mine. Then he pressed his lips against mine in a soft, sweet kiss that bordered on innocent.

Suddenly, I kissed him back. Then I shoved him away. My heart thudded and my eyes blurred with tears. What the hell was I doing? What was wrong with me? Guilt washed over me.

"Rosalie, I'm sorry...."

We weren't doing this. This was not happening and would never happen, again.

"Too many drinks." I swiped at tears. "We got caught up in a sweet moment." I patted his hand to show no harm had been done.

Something flickered in his eyes before he could hide the emotion behind a smile. Was that disappointment?

"You're right," he said. "Forgive me?"

"Of course. You want a cup of coffee?" I wanted anything that would take my mind off what had just happened.

"I'd love to, but I better get going," he said. "I've got an early set call tomorrow. Walk you to the door?"

"I'll settle for that," I said.

Holden got out of the car and came around to open my door.

"Thank you again. Tonight was wonderful." I pulled my keys from my purse.

"My pleasure. I'll call you tomorrow."

For a split second I stiffened as Holden pulled me into another hug, then I relaxed in his embrace. I turned the key in the lock, trying not to cry, as he strode to his car.

"It wasn't wrong, Rosalie," Holden called from his car.

I twisted and looked at him over my shoulder. "Holden...."

"That's all I'm going to say, okay?" he said. "It wasn't wrong."

Holden was my best friend. I could not lose him, but I also couldn't let this happen again. I pushed open the door and shut it behind me. Neither of my parents were up. Thank God for small favors.

I checked on Anthony, who slept soundly, then went to bed myself.

Sleep didn't come easy. Guilt nagged. How could I betray Sam? Despite the admonition, I couldn't stop thinking about Holden's kiss. My lips still tingled and tasted of Holden, like sweet red wine and a hint of salt. My heart swelled at the memory of his lips on mine.

Stop!

I would follow Sam's example and ignore the problem. But as hard as I tried to forget the kiss, I tossed and turned, torn between the ache in my heart that wanted Holden and the guilt that wracked me.

My dad left the following afternoon. Holden called, but kept the conversation short. Thankfully, everything felt normal, with no real traces left from the night before. My mom knew something was up but didn't push. Wonders never cease.

When Sam called later that day, I didn't tell him what happened, but hearing his voice brought on a fresh wave of guilt. I had no idea what kind of sentence Sam would get, and here I was with all this emotional turmoil that I couldn't manage to sort through.

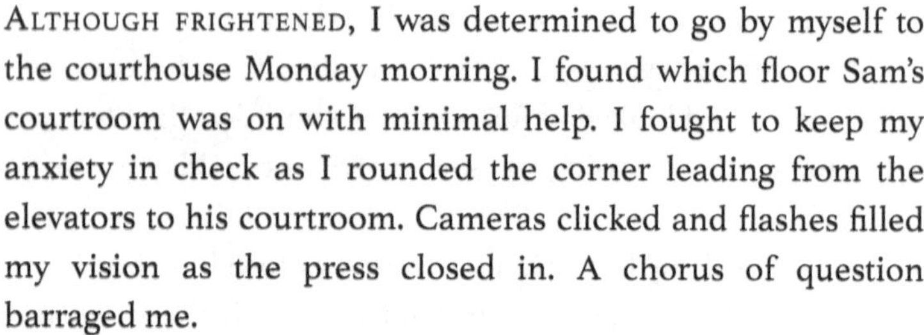

ALTHOUGH FRIGHTENED, I was determined to go by myself to the courthouse Monday morning. I found which floor Sam's courtroom was on with minimal help. I fought to keep my anxiety in check as I rounded the corner leading from the elevators to his courtroom. Cameras clicked and flashes filled my vision as the press closed in. A chorus of question barraged me.

"What do you think about the fact your husband broke parole?" one reporter shouted.

"Who's taking care of your son?" another cut in.

One stopped in my path. "Are you going to stand by your husband this time?"

My head spun. "Jesus! Don't you assholes have anything better to do?" I shouted.

They kept taking pictures and calling out questions until I reached the courtroom door and hurried inside. The door shut and cut off the noise.

I sat in a seat near the back of the courtroom. My stomach dropped when Sam emerged from a door to the left of the judge's seat. Dressed in an orange jumpsuit, handcuffed and shackled, my husband looked like a stranger. He had a three-day beard and looked gray and sick. I thought I would puke. Spotting me, he mouthed *I love you* then gave me a sad smile. My resolve not to cry in front of him nearly crumbled.

This was Sam's second appearance before the same judge for drug charges, and the judge wasn't pleased. Sam's probation officer was also in attendance. The judge recommended a sixty-day stay in rehab with a twist.

The judge locked eyes with Sam. "Mr. Urban, in order to get across to you the kind of path you're taking, I'm also ordering you to thirty days in the county jail, starting today.

Your sixty days in the rehab facility will immediately follow your release from Los Angeles County jail."

My head swam. *Three months.* He would miss Anthony's first Christmas. My heart twisted. My whole world was being ripped away from me. I watched numbly as the court officers led Sam out. He looked at me over his shoulder, face streaked with tears, and blew me a kiss. I couldn't stand. They called the next case, as I rocked back and forth and cried. I wanted my husband home.

On my way out ten minutes later, I prepared myself for the media that still circled outside like vultures. I made sure my face was dry and I kept my head down. This wasn't what I had signed up for. I thought I had gotten a fairy tale. Instead, my life was a nightmare wrapped in a pretty package.

When I arrived home, I walked through the front door and right into my mom's arms like I had as a small child. My head pounded and my stomach rejected anything that wasn't liquid. I hadn't realized how hard dealing with a Hollywood marriage would be, and I was grateful to have my mom.

Without my asking, she extended her stay a few more days. I almost laughed at how relieved I was when she told me. For as long as I could remember, I had been trying to get away from her, and now I was leaning on her for the first time since I was a child. Maybe I was beginning to understand her, just a little, anyway.

When Sam called later that afternoon, he couldn't speak for crying so hard. I felt so useless. I couldn't free him. I couldn't make his addiction go away. I couldn't even hold my husband while he fell apart.

TEN

As usual, Holden called later that night. Fresh tears fell as I told him the outcome of my phone call with Sam.

"Jesus, Rosalie. I'm sorry. Do you need anything?"

"Just my husband home."

"I wish I could make that happen," he said. "Listen, I wanted to tell you I leave next week for Florida for this new movie. They're filming on location."

"How long will you be gone?" The thought of not having Sam or Holden made my heart pound.

Holden sighed heavily. "Two months at least. Shitty timing. I'm sorry."

"Don't be sorry. Your job isn't to entertain me, Holden."

"But I like entertaining you. You and Anthony are family. Rosalie, I don't do anything because I have to. I do it because I want to. I enjoy your company. You're my best friend."

"That's really sweet. I needed that," I said.

"Then I've done my job."

I laughed. "You're my best friend, too. I don't know what I'd do without you."

"Ditto, kid. Dinner with me before I leave?"

I swiped at a tear that had pushed past my resolve. "Of course."

After we talked a while longer, Holden and I said goodbye, leaving me alone to untangle the way I felt about him and my marriage. I had to laugh. I was about to turn eighteen. Most eighteen-year-olds are just finishing high school. They're worrying about what college to go to, whether to live at home or in a dorm.

I was now a single parent, in a toxic and abusive marriage with a man I loved more than life itself. Said man was in jail, and my best friend was going to be away for two months. I was alone. We went from celebrating our anniversary and Thanksgiving to Sam being in jail in a matter of days. On November twenty-ninth, I sent my husband to work and by December second my world had collapsed.

Yes, I had wanted to be married at seventeen. Yes, I had wanted a baby. I hadn't known about all the extra bad shit that had come along for the ride.

But I had to suck it up. I didn't have time to lie down and wallow. My mom was leaving Thursday and, while I was glad she had been there to help me through my little breakdown, I was also glad she was leaving.

"You know it wouldn't hurt anything for you and the baby to come to Indiana while Sam's gone," she told me that night at dinner.

"We've been over this." I forked mashed potatoes into my mouth. "I'm not coming home. Sam needs me. He gets visits, and I am not taking that away from him."

Her mouth thinned. "Exactly what my grandson needs to see, his father through a glass window."

I took a deep breath and closed my eyes. "Not at the jail, Mother. At the rehab center."

"That's so much better?"

I hated leaving things like that between us, but my mother always pushed and pushed until a person exploded. I was relieved to drop her off at LAX the following morning.

Once home, the emptiness closed in on me. Thank God I had Anthony, or I would have lost my mind. The next day I signed us up for all the mommy and me classes I could find. If I was going to have to do this alone, then we were damn well going to have fun and make the best of a shitty situation.

HOLDEN HAD to be in Florida the following Monday, so he called to make plans to spend Sunday with us before he had to leave that evening. We hadn't seen each other since the night we went dancing. We'd only talked on the phone, and I wasn't sure what to expect.

Holden and I had such a strong bond. I was afraid that what had happened would affect our friendship. I didn't want anything to be awkward with us. I didn't know what I would do if I lost him.

By the time Sunday arrived, I chomped at the bit to get out of the house. Holden picked us up late morning. We went to lunch and decided to do some shopping. We were swarmed by photographers wherever we went, reminding me of the crowds on Christmas Eve.

But instead of a warm, nostalgic feeling, I was filled with panic. The photographers pushed in on all sides. A few hollered questions, but mainly they just pressed as close as possible while their cameras snapped and flashed.

As we tried to enter the little restaurant for lunch, they bunched impossibly closer. I hated them. I used to read the gossip magazines before I met and married Sam, but I never realized what celebrities went through.

I kept my head down and fought back tears. Holden turned Anthony's car seat away from them, trying to prevent their getting pictures. Finally, he put his other arm around me, and we left rather than be photographed while we sat inside and ate.

We went back to my place for delivery and movies. By that time, I realized I'd had no reason to be nervous. Holden never mentioned what happened between us. Being with him was as comfortable as an old blanket.

He stayed until well after Anthony had crashed for the night. We sat on the couch, drank wine, and talked.

"I really hate leaving you while Sam's gone," he said.

"I'm a big girl," I replied. "I'll be fine. Like I said, we aren't your responsibility. You have your own life."

"And like I told you, you are my family, therefore I do have a responsibility to you."

I laughed. "If I'm really your only source of entertainment, we seriously need to get you a wife."

"You may be my favorite source of entertainment, but I never said you were my only source of entertainment." He waggled his brows.

I rolled my eyes. "Do you ever think about getting married?"

He hesitated. "I've thought about it, sure. I've even come close once or twice."

"Then why is a catch like you still single?"

"I don't know about being a catch. I guess I've just never found the right girl." His expression clouded.

"She'll be one lucky girl, that's for sure," I said. "You'll find her when the time is right."

Holden chuckled. "When the time is finally right, I have no doubt in my mind." He checked his watch. "Damn, I really need to get going."

I walked him to the door, where he wrapped me in a big bear hug. "You sure you're going to be okay?" he asked.

"I'll be fine. Call me when you get there," I whispered.

"But of course," he said in a cheesy French accent.

I closed the door and tears well up again, but I refused to cry. I had to be an adult. If this was the hand life dealt me, then I damn sure was going to play it.

THE FIRST VISIT with Sam a few days later broke both our hearts. I left Anthony with Joey and prepared myself as best as I could. Our visit was between a glass window. I couldn't hold Sam. I couldn't touch him. My heart dropped when he came through the door to the visitation area. His ashen pallor accentuated his gaunt cheeks. Deep, dark circles framed his eyes and a bruise encircled his left cheek. We each picked up the phone in order to hear each other.

"Oh, Sam, what happened?" I choked on a small sob.

He laughed darkly. "I'm paying for being a celebrity. Being in general population has been so much fun."

Even though I had sworn I wouldn't, I couldn't help but cry. Sam looked like death and seeing him terrified me.

"I'm so happy to see you. Knowing I would see you today has been the only thing keeping me going." Sam choked back tears as he pressed his hand against the glass that separated us.

I put my hand against his. As long as I live, I will never forget the feel of the cold glass that separated us or the torture of being so close but not being able to touch him.

"I'm so sorry, Rosalie. I'm sorry for everything. I'd sell my soul to change what I've done, for this to have never happened and to be home with you and Anthony." Sam dropped his head his shoulders shook with sobs.

"Then change things this time. Please, Sam. Don't let this happen again," I said softly.

Sam lifted his head and nodded. "I will. I swear to God I am done with this. I just want to be home with you guys."

"We want you home."

"Anthony won't remember me."

"Of course, he will," I assured him.

"Don't bring him here, Rosalie, please. I know he won't remember, but I will. I never want him to see me like this."

I nodded. I had no intention of bringing my son to see his father in jail.

"Are you okay?" Sam asked. "I've been so busy wallowing in self-pity, I haven't even bothered to ask you."

"I miss you. The house feels so empty without you. I'm okay. I'm trying to be, anyway. Anthony keeps me busy. The nights are the hardest. I pretend you're filming somewhere, and you'll be home the next day. But I don't sleep well without you."

"I'm so sorry."

"Then make your sobriety work this time, Sam, please." My voice cracked.

"I promise. I'm going to get through this nightmare, and then I swear I'm going to make all this up to you guys. I swear I'll be everything you and Anthony need."

The guard stepped forward to let Sam know our time was up. "I love you, Rosalie, more than anything." He kissed the tips of his fingers then held them to the glass. I did the same. I lingered while the guard led Sam back through the door, then I left.

～

AFTER THAT FIRST VISIT, I experienced severe depression. I started to recover, but after the second visit, the depression returned, and I recognized the cycle would begin anew with each visit. Christmas was two weeks away, and I hadn't bought presents or even attempted to decorate let alone put up a tree.

Life went on, though. The world didn't stop just because my husband was in jail. Therefore, I had to go on, too. I adjusted as best as I could, and something amazing started to happen.

Slowly, I found my independence. First, I braved driving in LA. I got lost several times, but eventually I figured things out on my own. I had no choice. Joey worked almost nonstop. Sam was gone. Holden was gone. The days before cell phones and GPS were quite the adventure.

On my third visit with Sam, I handled myself with less emotion and decided to make that my practice. We still cried, but we focused more on when he was getting out and how we would get through treatment instead of how sad the situation was or how we wished we could change things.

Finally, I found that I enjoyed being alone, at least some of the time. I enjoyed doing what I wanted and how I wanted.

FIVE BEFORE CHRISTMAS, Holden surprised us with a visit. He wore a Santa hat and cheesy grin on his face.

"Ho! Ho! Ho!" He dragged in a seven-foot tall artificial Christmas tree through the doorways. I couldn't believe he was there or that he had remembered I was allergic to real evergreens. Anthony's face lit up when he saw Holden.

"What are you doing here?" I threw my arms around his neck.

"I thought I would surprise my two favorite people."

"I just talked to you last night," I said. "This was definitely not expected."

"All part of my plan. You look amazing." He released me.

Anthony squealed from the living room. He was just discovering he had a voice and babbled all the time.

"That can't be my boy," Holden exclaimed striding into the living room. "He's doubled in size in less than a month." Holden scooped Anthony up and tickled his belly. Anthony giggled and grabbed fistfuls of Holden's shoulder length blonde hair.

"There's more stuff in the car," Holden said.

"Holden...." I began.

"What? Filming is stalled right now, problems with the set structure so they gave us a week off from shooting for the holidays, and I wanted to make sure my godson's first Christmas is amazing."

"Your being here would have been sufficient," I said.

"No, it wouldn't have," he said in a baby voice to Anthony. "We have to make Christmas special, don't we? Mommy's slacking, so Uncle Holden got a tree and decorations and presents. Yes, he did."

"Hey!" I cried in mock anger. "I'm not slacking. I just haven't started yet."

"Uh huh. You're letting everything get to you. The Rosalie I know would've had this place looking like the North Pole two weeks ago."

"Yeah, well...." I trailed off.

"So, I brought some Christmas cheer, sue me."

Laughing, I rolled my eyes.

Holden played with Anthony a while longer, then began bringing everything inside. Overboard didn't cover everything Holden did. He made three trips to his car and brought not only the tree but decorations for the tree and the house and more toys than Anthony would ever play with.

"This is way too much." I scanned the pile of boxes.

"You hush. Let me enjoy this," Holden said.

I started dinner while Holden put up the tree. I needed something to get me in the holiday spirit, and his visit certainly did the trick. By the time I got dinner done and the table set, Holden had the tree up and strung with glimmering lights.

"How beautiful! Thank you so much." I sat on the arm of the couch to admire his handiwork.

"I'm nowhere near done, but I wanted you to hang the first ornament." Holden held out a red box.

"Oh, Holden," I breathed as I opened the box.

Inside was a teddy bear riding a blue rocking horse, a 'first Christmas' ornament with Anthony's name and date of birth inscribed.

Anthony

4-24-1991

First Christmas

ELEVEN

"Do you like it?" Holden asked.

"I love it. This is amazing." I hugged him, then hung the ornament on the tree front and center.

Holden put his arm around me, and we got lost in the moment and the lights. Despite my happiness, I missed Sam.

Holden gave me a squeeze. "I'd do anything for you, kid."

"I know. Let's eat" I scooped Anthony up and hurried into the kitchen before I could crying.

"Did I upset you?" Holden took his seat opposite me.

"God, no." I laughed. "I'm sorry. I'm just emotional with everything."

"I just wanted to check. I don't ever want to upset you. You've had enough of that."

"That's the truth. To be honest, I don't think you could even if you tried."

He gave me a wry smile. "I doubt that. But as long as you're happy, I'm happy."

In reality, I was confused. Holden meant the world to me. Though I didn't want to admit the truth, sometimes when I was with him, I completely forgot Sam. I had to be the worst wife on the face of the earth. But I felt safe with Holden, and I felt loved.

I was married, and my husband was going through a crisis. These feelings weren't okay. But I refused to lose my relationship with Holden. I had to keep my mouth shut and ignore those feelings.

After dinner, I put Anthony to bed. When I came back down, the lights were low and the tree was lit up. Holden handed me a glass of wine, and we relaxed on the couch after I turned on the baby monitor. The tree twinkled in the low light. Holden put his arm across the back of the couch, behind me but not quite around me. There it was. That feeling of home and warmth and love. We sat like that for a long time, watching the lights dance on the walls and sipping our wine.

At some point, I leaned over and laid my head against Holden's chest and closed my eyes. The next thing I knew Holden was gently shaking me awake. My eyes snapped open.

I bolted upright. "Oh hell, I'm sorry."

Holden chuckled. "Don't be. I fell out, too. It's late. I'm gonna go."

"What time is it?"

"Almost three in the morning," he replied.

"Wow. You might as well stay, it's so late. Not like I don't have a spare bedroom."

He hesitated. "Are you sure?"

"Of course. There's no reason for you to be out driving so late when you're just gonna be back here tomorrow," I said.

Holden's lips curled into a soft grin. He started to take my hand but stopped himself. I gave a small sigh of relief. The hour was too late, and in that moment, I didn't trust myself. But that didn't stop my heart from pounding.

Without words, we climbed the stairs. The spare bedroom

was adjacent from my bedroom. The bedroom I shared with Sam.

Holden paused in the door to the spare bedroom. "Tonight was great, Rosalie. Thank you for being in my life."

My heart jumped into my throat. "Is this enough, though? Our friendship?" The words were out of my mouth before I could stop them.

Stop it! Shut up!

Holden's expression softened. "I'll take what you can give."

I nodded, then closed the door to our bedroom and leaned heavily against it. My life was a complete fucking mess. I loved Sam. I did. At least that's what I told myself. I was also terrified of him. But I had said for better or for worse, and I didn't run when things got hard.

I also loved Holden, but in a much different way. He was safe. He was calm and steady. His moods didn't change at the bat of an eye. I wasn't terrified of him. I climbed into bed and the war inside my head raged until I fell into a fitful sleep.

I SLEPT late into the next morning. When I finally looked at the clock on the bedside table, it was almost nine-thirty. I flew out of bed in a panic. Unless he was sick, Anthony never slept past eight.

My pounding heart calmed when I heard Holden's voice and Anthony's giggles from downstairs. I reached the living room and relief flooded me at the sight of Holden playing with Anthony on the couch

"Good morning, Mommy," Holden said.

"You didn't have to get him. Thank you."

Holden shrugged. "I thought it'd be nice for you to sleep in. I figured the last time you did that was before this bundle of joy made his appearance." Holden gently bounced Anthony up and down on his knee. I sat down beside them. My son smiled and held his arms out to me.

Holden handed him over and grinned. "What?"

"Nothing. Just seeing you with him. Coffee?"

"Is that really a question?"

Holden patted my leg. "Coming right up."

WE SPENT the day putting up decorations. Holden put on Christmas music and, with a shy smile, thrust a box of ornaments into my hands.

"Deck the halls!" he sang, and pointed me at the bare tree.

I shrugged, definitely not feeling the whole holiday thing. An hour into Bing Crosby and listening to Holden sing softly under his breath brought out all the warm fuzzies. By the time we were done, my house and, more importantly, my soul were covered in Christmas magic.

"We're going out for your birthday," Holden told me.

"You don't have to do that."

He shook his head. "No, I don't. I want to. I already have everything booked, and my mom offered to watch Anthony."

I frowned. "I don't want to pawn him off on your mom."

"Please, she adores him. My mom couldn't love Anthony more if he were her grandchild."

I laughed. "Well, she is more of a grandma than Sam's mother."

"Exactly," he said. "She watched Sam grow up, so any child of his is always going to be family."

"I really hope you didn't go to any trouble over me," I warned.

"Nothing for you is ever trouble. This is a milestone. You're turning eighteen."

"I think my milestones were over when Sam got me emancipated."

"Well, this is still a big deal, and we're going to celebrate." He winked.

Holden stayed for dinner but left before my nightly call with Sam. Sam was in a decent mood, so the conversation was a less emotional than they had been. I felt guilty, nonetheless.

Sam already had a few projects lined up for his release from rehab. I guess the old saying that any publicity is good publicity was true. He had more job offers while he was in jail than he had before his drug use and arrests had come to light.

That week I finally started my Christmas shopping. I would host my own little dinner at my house with Anthony, Joey, and Holden. Thankfully, my parents were both staying in Indiana. Sam got to have an extra visit on Christmas, and ours would be first thing Christmas morning.

THE TWENTY-SECOND OF DECEMBER, I turned eighteen. Holden picked me up that evening, and we left Anthony with his mom. Holden surprised me by taking me back to the restaurant in Long Beach we had gone to when Sam was arrested.

A few people, including our waiter, recognized Holden, but unlike in LA, they left us alone. There was no mob of people snapping pictures as we ate. It was just a normal night out.

While we waited for our meal, Holden held my hand. "Happy birthday, Rosalie."

I gave his hand a squeeze. "Thank you. This means so much to me."

"Got you something." Holden gave me his goofy grin.

"You went to enough trouble," I protested.

"Hush." He reached under the table, brought out a gift bag, and handed it to me.

He had to have had this already planned because I didn't see him carry anything inside. By the bag's weight, I knew it contained books. I took them out and unwrapped the first one. It was a hardback first edition of *The Thorn Birds* by Colleen McCullough. I had read that book twenty times.

"Oh my God, Holden, thank you so much." I ran a hand over the cover.

"Open the next one," he urged. He was more excited than I was.

The next book was a 1933 printing of *The Three Musketeers* by Alexandre Dumas. I ran my fingertips across the lettering on the cover.

I had been obsessed with that book since the first time I read it in middle school. There was talk about a new Musketeer movie being made, the possibility of casting coming as early the week after New Year's Day. I thought Holden would make the perfect Athos.

This had to have cost Holden a thousand dollars, or more.

"I don't have any words," I stammered.

"Do you like it?"

"I love it. No one's ever done anything like this for me."

"I knew you'd love it."

"Thank you," I breathed.

"The look on your face is all the thanks I need," he replied. "Happy birthday, honey."

I choked back tears. Holden and I had many conversations, and he seemed to remember everything I said. I doubted Sam knew my favorite color.

"Holden...I...."

He patted my hand. "You don't have to say anything. Just dance with me."

I did. That evening floated by.

WHEN WE ARRIVED BACK at Holden's parents' house after one in the morning, of course, Anthony was long conked out.

"There's no sense in waking him up and dragging him out," Louise, Holden's mother, said. "I set up his portable crib in the small guest room. You might as well get some sleep, too."

I was tipsy from the wine and drunk on happiness. "Thank you so much," I told her, and followed Holden upstairs.

We peeked at Anthony. Sound asleep.

As we entered the guest bedroom across from Anthony's room, Holden pulled me into a hug. "Did you enjoy yourself?" he asked.

"This was the best birthday I ever had."

He rested his chin on the top of my head. "I'm glad I could make you happy."

"Always," I said.

Slowly, his arms loosened around me and he stepped away. "You know, I—" He stopped.

"What?" I pressed.

"Nothing. Just a dumb idea. Never mind."

I sat on the bed and pulled him down next to me. "No, tell me. Might turn out better than you think."

He seemed to fumble for words, and in the dim light, I realized his eyes were shiny with tears.

"What's wrong?" I brushed a piece of hair from his eyes. He caught my hand and kissed it. "Holden, what is going on? You're scaring me."

"I'm sorry," he said in a thick voice. "We'll talk about this later." He kissed me on the forehead and rose.

"Holden," I said sharply. "You're not leaving until you tell me what's going on."

"I can't."

"Since when?" I demanded.

He met my eyes. His lips parted, and I thought he was going to speak but instead he swept me up and into his arms and kissed me. My body hummed to life and his lips trembled against mine, eager and waiting. I kissed him back. I could give a hundred excuses why I didn't push him away. Instead, I kissed him because I wanted him.

He was my safe place. He was where my heart went late at night when the day was done and I was alone. I wrapped my arms around his neck, knowing I needed to end this right now.

When he finally pulled away, my arms were still around his neck. We pressed our foreheads together and clung to each other in silence.

"I'm sorry," he whispered.

"I know." I was ashamed of myself, but I couldn't let him go.

"This is not wrong, Rosalie. I know you think so, but he doesn't deserve you. I can't stay away from you."

"I know. I can't stay away from you either. But Holden, we can't.... Stay with me," I whispered. "Just stay."

Without a word, he took off his suit jacket and draped it across the dresser. We lay in the bed, chest to chest, with my head nestled on his arm and my face buried in his neck. I fell asleep while he stroked my hair.

We'd deal with the repercussions in the morning.

∾

Anthony's baby babble woke us to morning sunlight streaming through the window. We were still tangled in each other's arms, but Holden wouldn't meet my eyes.

"Why won't you look at me?" I asked.

"I was afraid I'd wake up and find you gone. Or you'd be upset, or both, and you'd end our friendship."

"I can't lose you," I whispered.

Holden brushed my bangs from my forehead. "Same, kiddo."

I searched his eyes. "Even if I can't give you more?"

"No," he said. "Just until you're ready."

I smacked his arm playfully. "You're an ass. What if I'm never ready? I do love Sam, you know."

"You think you do. And if you never want me, then I still have great memories with my best friend."

"We can't let this happen again," I said.

"I know." Holden kissed me. "Last one," he whispered. "For now, anyway."

Anthony's babble had turned into angry squawks, so I was saved from answering. I felt guilty for not feeling guilty. I loved Sam, I truly did, but I was so tired of his meanness and selfishness. The only thing Sam was teaching me was how to live without him.

I also loved Holden, but I wasn't going to admit that this was a romantic love. I had to bury that as deep as I possibly could because having those kinds of feelings were wrong.

I argued with myself while I got Anthony fed and changed. For now, Holden and I put the evening behind us and pretended nothing happened.

Pretending was a game I had gotten really good at playing.

TWELVE

On Christmas Eve, I started my first tradition with Anthony. He got new Christmas pajamas, chocolate milk, and a new Christmas movie. He wasn't really interested in the movie at his age, but still we snuggled on a pallet of blankets I'd made on the living room floor and fell asleep.

My Christmas visit with Sam was at ten in the morning. I made Joey stay with Anthony and the ham while I went. I both dreaded and looked forward to being near my husband. I needed to see Sam, keep him close to my heart, and stop being stupid.

Sam looked a little better, but he had lost more weight.

"Hi, baby," he said softly.

Guilt washed over me in waves, and I burst into tears. Never again would I allow myself to get caught up in my make-believe world with Holden.

"I know, Rosalie. I am so sorry for the way things are," Sam said, and I was thankful that he mistook my distress for missing him. It wasn't a total lie. "This is the last time I'll be telling you 'Merry Christmas' through a glass window."

"I hope so, Sam. I need you. I don't think I can take much more of this. I need you to get and stay sober."

"I'm going to. I promise. I know you may not think so, but I do love you." Tears swam in Sam's eyes.

My stomach clenched. I loved Sam. I wanted the life that we were supposed to have.

"I love you, too, Sam. I love you so much."

We had only an hour, so I switched the subject and showed Sam pictures of Anthony. That put him in a better mood. After a tearful goodbye, I buried the sadness and went home to finish our Christmas celebration. I was determined to make our small gathering special.

HOLDEN HAD ALREADY ARRIVED when I returned. He seemed to be burying what happened between us that night at his folk's house just as deeply as I was.

All in all, Christmas was a success. I probably took a thousand pictures and sent Joey home with enough food for a week.

Holden was leaving to finish shooting in Florida the following morning, which meant I would be on my own again. But this time I didn't mind as much. I needed the time alone and the distance from Holden to get myself and my thoughts in order.

Sam was released from LA county jail on December thirtieth and was immediately admitted to the rehab center to serve his sixty days, which stretched before me into oblivion.

My first visit with Sam in rehab was hard. Anthony refused to go to him. He didn't know who Sam was anymore. Without the drugs in Sam's system, I'm sure his scent had changed or something. Whatever was different about him, Anthony wanted nothing to do with Sam. I think that more than anything else got to Sam the most.

"Christ, my own kid doesn't even remember me," Sam cried. "This shit is done, I swear."

Over the next eight weeks, Anthony warmed up to Sam. I think what helped the most during those eight weeks was that Holden was gone. Sam had been so in and out of his little life so far and, until now, Holden had been a constant male figure in Anthony's world.

Sam came home the first week of March, and life was an adjustment for us both. I was used to coming and going as I pleased, and he was used to being monitored and restricted.

The first three weeks were okay. We had a few rocky patches here and there, but I excused Sam's dark moods as his way of coping and processing the events of the last year.

While I wasn't worried about his using again because he had random drug tests, I still couldn't pin down exactly what was going on with him. Sometimes Sam would lock himself in his office for hours at a time and refuse to respond. During one of these times I got fed up and took Anthony shopping for his birthday party.

Sam insisted on Anthony's first birthday being a big blow out, yet here we were with a week to go and nothing was done. By this time, I was accustomed to getting things done. I didn't think Sam would mind my taking care of the details.

Anthony had conked out on the way home and I was juggling his car seat and the food I'd picked up on the way home when I stepped through the door. Sam was sitting on the couch with the curtains closed and the lights off.

"Hey, Hun," I said. "I grabbed dinner. Why are you sitting in the dark? You okay?"

Sam remained motionless and watched me. Anthony was

snoozing hard, so I left him in the car seat and sat him on the floor next to Sam.

"You want me to fix you a plate?" I asked.

Giving me a ghost of a smile, Sam extended his hand. I sat the food on the coffee table and put my hand in his. Sam yanked me onto his lap hard.

"Ow, Sam," I cried.

He grabbed a handful of my hair and forced me to look up at him. "Where the hell have you been?"

"Getting things for Anthony's party. Let go of me, you're hurting me!"

"Shut up. You've been gone for four hours shopping?"

"Yes."

His grip tightened, and he had one of my arms pinned behind me.

"Where is everything then?" he demanded.

I stared, dumbfounded. He'd been home only a few weeks, and we were already back to this shit?

"In the car," I snapped. "I wanted to bring Anthony in first. Sam, you've got to let go of me. You're hurting me."

He released me. I jumped to my feet and scurried backwards. "What's wrong with you?" My arm ached and I fought tears.

"I'm not the one who has a problem, Rosalie, darling, that's you." Sam stood, his mouth curled up in a sickening sneer beneath a smoldering glare.

My heart dropped.

I knew what I was in for.

"You've had way too much freedom while I was gone," he said in a chilling voice. "All you do is run around and spend money. What kind of wife are you? You're not here taking care of me or even thinking of me."

"Someone has to get food and household stuff, honey," I

said. I realized he was slowly inching toward me.

Anthony sighed in his sleep, and Sam stopped to look at him. I mentally plotted a path from me to the baby to the door. Despair washed over me. Sam stood between me and our son.

Sam's attention returned to me. "You don't tell me when you're leaving."

I had, but now wasn't the time. "I'm sorry," I stammered. I doubted anything I said was going to defuse the situation.

"Who were you with?" he demanded.

I looked at Sam hopelessly. "What?"

He growled low in his chest, then took two quick steps and stood in front of me. I threw up my hands in an effort to protect myself. Sam's backhanded blow struck me across my cheek. My head snapped to the left.

"Don't play stupid with me!" he shouted.

I bit back my cry. Anthony jumped, but settled back into sleep.

"You're always running off somewhere." Sam stepped closer. "Who is he ?"

"There is no one. Only you." I choked back tears.

Sam backed me against the wall. He put an arm on each side of me and brought his face to within an inch of mine. "Don't fucking lie to me."

"Sam, I'm not lying."

He closed his eyes and shook his head. "Rosalie, Rosalie, Rosalie...."

"I haven't been with anyone but you." I cupped his cheek with my trembling hand.

He slapped my hand away. "Not even Holden?"

I drew a sharp breath. That was enough evidence for Sam to convict me. Sam's seized my throat. We fell to the floor, him on top of me.

"You fucking bitch!" With one hand still around my throat,

he slapped me across the right side then the left side of my face. He wrapped his second hand around my throat and squeezed. "How long?"

I clawed at his fingers and wheezed for breath. Anthony began shrieking at the top of his lungs.

"Everything's all right, buddy," Sam sang calmly to Anthony. He loosened his grip on my throat, and I gasped for air. "Mommy's been a bad girl. Daddy's teaching her a lesson," Sam continued in the same singsong voice.

Please don't let him kill me, I begged God.

"How long?" Sam demanded again.

"Never," I croaked.

"You're a fucking liar!" Sam decked me.

My nose broke with an audible crunch and I cried out. Suddenly, Sam's weight lifted off me. He stood and walked over to where Anthony lay screaming in his car seat.

I coughed and tried to breathe as a crimson river poured from my broken nose. Spots raced across my vision. Sam picked up Anthony and gently bounced him, consoling him as if the last minute hadn't happened at all.

I must have lost consciousness for a little while because the next time I opened my eyes, Anthony lay on the floor with a bottle. I didn't immediately see Sam. I laid still and listened for him. After a moment, the front door opened and the rustle of bags mingled with the approach of feet.

I tried to sit up, setting off a shock of pain throughout my body. A moment later, Sam came into view at my side and he extended a hand to me. He looked right through me with blank eyes, like he didn't even see me.

As much as I didn't want his help, I took his hand and allowed him to pull me onto my feet. I stumbled to the couch and collapsed onto the cushions. My head swam. I closed my eyes and breathed deeply to avoid passing out again. After several minutes, Sam pulled me into a standing position. He kept an arm around me as I fought for balance.

"See, buddy. I told you Mommy just needed a nap. Go clean yourself up," he hissed into my ear.

I stumbled into the bathroom and leaned heavily on the sink as I stared at my reflection in the mirror. Deep purple bruises already formed around the bridge of my nose and under my eyes. My nose was definitely broken. I just hoped it didn't heal too crookedly.

I soaked a rag in cold water and cleaned the blood off my face and neck. Then I took a clean cloth, wetted it, and pressed the soft fabric gently to the bridge of my nose. I tried not to cry as relief and pain warred for dominance. I didn't want to think about how bad blowing my nose was going to hurt.

I wanted to tell myself I couldn't believe he'd broken my nose, but I could. Deep purple bruises were already setting in around my neck. That meant I'd be wearing turtleneck shirts and scarves for the next month.

I FELT like I had been standing in the bathroom for hours, when really I'd been in there maybe twenty minutes before I could to force myself to return to the living room. Sam had warmed up the Chinese food I'd brought home and set up our TV trays in the living room. Anthony played nearby on his blanket.

With a wide smile, Sam patted the empty spot next to him. I didn't want to be in the same house with him, let alone sit next to him, but to refuse was dangerous.

"That's my good girl. See? Lesson learned. No more taking off, right?" He spoke to me like I was a child who had just gotten out of timeout.

"Yes, Sam."

"To avoid any further situations, you'll have a time limit when you leave the house."

There was no apology, no acknowledgment of the beating he'd dealt out. Sam smiled and stroked my leg and laughed along with a sitcom like nothing had happened. I ate little and said even less.

That night after Anthony was asleep, Sam wanted to have sex. I let him. Every moment hurt and made me feel like I was going to throw up. Each time I cried out or whimpered, Sam took that as encouragement. My skin crawled with his every touch. I loved Sam so much, but I couldn't stand the thought of him near me. When he was finally finished, he rolled onto his side, put his arm around me, and pulled me against him.

I lay awake for a long time. I needed to leave. But I was much too afraid to take a chance that he wouldn't carry out the threat of forcing me to come back, and that was only if he didn't kill me.

The man had bought my emancipation along with our marriage. there was no way in hell I was risking a custody battle.

I woke early the next morning to the smell of bacon and coffee. Gingerly, I sat up, giving myself a few minutes for the dizziness to pass. Once I confirmed that Anthony still slept, I made my way downstairs. On the kitchen table sat a huge bouquet of white lilies and a couple of small black velvet jewelry boxes.

"Hi." Sam handed me a cup of coffee.

"Hi," I answered.

"Rosalie, I'm sorry. I don't even remember what happened."

I took the coffee and sat down.

"How bad is the pain?" he asked.

"Hurts like a bitch," I muttered. Even sipping my coffee hurt.

Slowly, Sam approached mem. When he tried to put his arms around me, I flinched. At his sharp intake of breath, I braced.

"You're afraid of me," he said. "Oh my God, I'm so sorry."

Sam sank to his knees, put his head in my lap, and cried so hard that his body shook. An Academy Award performance if I ever saw one. I sat rigid in my chair. My stomach turned. I forgave him. A tale as old as time. I didn't see any other choice. I had to forgive him.

Sam stood and took the chair opposite me. He clasped my hand between his. "I need help, Rosalie. This is not drugs, this is me. I don't know why I do the things I do or what gets in my head. I'm so sorry. Maybe the shrink at rehab was right."

Sam's eyes were bright as he searched my face. I raised an eyebrow at him but remained silent.

"At rehab they said I was bi-polar," he went on. "They had me on some different medications, but I stopped taking them when I came home. I didn't really think I needed them."

I stared. This was the first I'd heard of any of this. I didn't know what to think.

"I'll make an appointment with the doctor," he said. "I'll do anything to make sure this doesn't happen again."

"Me too," I said flatly.

I had wished so often for things to change that I was numb to any hope that the abuse would stop.

Tears trickled down his cheeks. Sam leaned over to kiss me. "This is absolutely nothing you did. It's me, all me. I'm the great fuck up. Please don't leave me. You have every reason to, but please don't. I'd kill myself without you and Anthony."

"I'm not," I replied.

Sam wiped the back of his hand across his eyes. He went to the stove to fix me a plate, but I just stared down at the plate. Eggs, sausage, and toast. Normally these were my favorites, but the smell made me nauseous.

"I've got something for the pain, but you need to eat first," he said.

I picked at the food while he went upstairs, but what little I ate sat like cement in my stomach. Sam returned and handed me two white pills.

"What are they?" I asked.

"Vicodin. They'll help, but they'll probably knock you on your ass."

I accepted the pills and knocked them back with some juice. I didn't ask where he got them or why he had them. I didn't care. And after they kicked in, I really didn't care. Sam took care of Anthony, and I drifted in and out of a restless sleep most of the day.

By Anthony's birthday party, my bruises had faded to a yellow and green mess. This was problematic not only because of our guests but also because Sam was allowing a magazine to photograph the party and run an interview with him.

To remedy the situation, Sam had a makeup artist he'd worked with come to the house to fix my face. The guy was older and very nice. Sam gave him some story about Anthony rearing his head back and head-butting me in the nose. The guy chuckled, said something about kids being kids, and gave me a smile that didn't reach his eyes. He knew exactly what had happened but was too much of a professional to comment.

The film grade crap disguised the bruises. The only evidence of the beating was a little swelling around my nose and under my eyes and a slightly crooked nose. Accessorizing my dress with a pretty scarf to cover the bruises on my neck, I prayed that once the pictures were filtered and airbrushed, no one would be able to tell anything.

The one person who did notice was Holden. He pulled me aside in the kitchen. "What's wrong with your face?"

"Nothing."

His eyes narrowed. "Bullshit. Your nose wasn't bent when last I saw you. What happened?"

I glanced around for Sam. All I needed was for him to see Holden and me alone in the kitchen. Fortunately, Sam posed for pictures in the living room, his back to us.

"Nothing. It was an accident. Leave it alone, okay?" I tried to walk around him, but Holden blocked my way.

"He fucking hit you, didn't he?"

"Holden, please." I blinked back tears.

"I warned him." Holden started for the living room, and I grabbed his arm.

"Don't you dare," I hissed.

"Rosalie, this has to stop."

"I know. He's going to get help. But you charging in there in front of the cameras and God isn't going to make anything stop. The only thing that's going to do is hurt me and Anthony."

His expression dropped. "How long are you going to let this go on? When will this stop? When he kills you?"

"Now is not the time for this. Please, I'm begging you." I was damn near in hysterics.

"I don't want a phone call telling me you're dead because he went too far," he hissed.

"Please, Holden, don't do this here. Not now," I begged.

"Goddamn it, fine." He clenched his fists. "But that son of a bitch has one coming from me. I'm just waiting for the day it finally clicks in your head."

I didn't know what to say. Holden moved aside and let me pass, but for the rest of the party he interacted as little as possible with Sam. Whenever our eyes met, he looked sad.

SAM'S DOCTOR confirmed the bi-polar diagnosis and put him on medication. The improvement was almost immediate. When Sam took his medication, life was good. When he didn't take it, not so much.

My life going forward consisted of Sam on and off the meds, on and off the drugs. I experienced happy, loving moments that could quickly transition into death threats and beatings for not having dinner on time or being gone five minutes longer than I had told him I'd be. Even something as simple as not having fresh towels in the bathroom could end in tearful apologies.

Other than Holden, I began isolating myself even more than I already did. Joey's life had become just as busy as mine, he'd been promoted at the factory and his relationship with Paul had turned serious, so our visits had tapered off over the last year. Never knowing when I'd have bruises or a broken bone, I made excuses most of the time to avoid Joey finding anything out.

Vicky usually flew in once or twice a year. Most of the time we knew in advance when she was coming and I would take great pains to make sure Sam was happy and content in the days leading up to her visit. For whatever reason when she did have a trip planned Sam went on his best behavior.

Sam completed his six month probation requirements and

passed all his drug tests without incident, though how I'll never know. During this time, I went from dutiful and loving wife who was willing to do anything to save her marriage to a detached stranger.

Holden visited frequently and, if he happened to notice a new bruise, he made no comment but gave me sad looks. My only peace and sanity were when Sam was filming away from home. My only real safety when he was home was when the lawn crew or the cleaning service were here. As of late, there had been way too many nannies and maids writing tell-all books about the celebrities they worked for. Sam was always on his best and nicest behavior when they were around.

I prayed often and I couldn't understand why God didn't answer. I prayed every night for God to make Sam happy, to fix me and make me a better wife. For Him to help me to not make Sam angry. But no matter what I did, the cycle always repeated.

On the morning of June 13, 1994, I sat in the kitchen drinking a cup of coffee and listening to the radio. With a horrible knot in my stomach, I heard about the murders of Nicole Brown Simpson and Ronald Goldman for the first time.

I was just as captivated by the case as the entire nation. Five days later, O.J. Simpson was charged in the double murder. For the first time since the 1992 riots, I watched the news 24/7. When the claims of domestic violence along with the police reports and pictures of a badly beaten Nicole came out, I was sick. But I almost felt relief in knowing that I wasn't the only woman married to a famous, wealthy man who was violent enough to take a beating too far.

During the middle of the trial, Holden visited. We watched the coverage and listened to the shocking 911 recordings. I had a swollen lip and a fresh bruise across my face.

"Do you know how terrified I am that one morning I'm going to wake up to a news story about you?" Holden's voice was soft and tight.

"Sam would never—"

"You really believe that? After all this time, after all the beatings, do you really, truly believe that?"

I didn't.

When the verdict of not guilty was handed down, I had the paralyzing realization that I would never get out of my marriage. I scoffed at the news commentators stating that if you were being abused to seek help, to find a way out. What would be the point? For me, that trial proved that famous, wealthy men would always be allowed a pass. OJ was practically a spokesman for men like my husband.

All the times Sam had hit me, I believed beyond any doubt that if I tried to leave he would kill me. Sometimes, when things calmed down, I'd lie in the dark next to him, mentally playing this fantasy of leaving. After the OJ trial, I stopped doing that. My husband had bought my emancipation. He'd bought our marriage.

Vicky called from London the day after the verdict. "I assume you saw the outcome of the trial?" she asked.

I picked up the phone from the living room side table. "Yes," I answered wearily. Sam was in a mood and I was attempting to talk as quietly as I could.

"Do you know how terrified I am of you being next? Every time the phone rings in the middle of the night I think it's Holden telling me Sam's killed you. Rosalie, I'm scared for you and Anthony."

Standing in the living room I did my best to nonchalantly check for Sam before responding. "I am too. We're on another bad cycle. His moods are beyond sporadic," I whispered into the phone.

"Oh, Rosalie," Vicky choked back tears.

"Who the hell are you talking to?" Sam demanded from the stairs.

"It's Vicky." I fought to keep the panic from rising in my voice.

"Uh huh, sure," Sam yanked the cordless phone out of my hand. "Hello?"

"You're such a pig!" I heard Vicky roar.

"And you're a peach. Rosalie's busy right now. Bye" He clicked off the call.

We stared at one another there for several seconds. For me that might as well have been hours. Sam moved impossibly fast and was suddenly inches from my face. I braced myself and flinched.

"The lawn guys will be here anytime. Are you going to change out of your nightgown or are you a whore for them, too?" he demanded.

"I'm going to get dressed now. I just wanted to start your coffee first."

Sam grunted, then spun and headed for the kitchen. I hurried upstairs to get dressed. After that, any doubt that Sam would take things too far, disappeared.

He would. He could. And he'd get away with it.

As if to prove the point, in the late summer of 1996, Sam was outed in an affair with a young actress working on his current project. Several tabloids and magazines featured pictures and one even included an exclusive interview with the young, slim pretty brunette. When I confronted Sam with the pictures and the interviews, he simply shrugged and locked himself in his office for half the day.

When he finally came out of his office for dinner, I brought up the subject of divorce and got a black eye and a busted lip for the effort.

THIRTEEN

Everything came to a head on a weekend in early September 1996. Anthony was four. Early that Friday morning, I awoke to blaring rock music streaming from Sam's office. I flung the door open, walked in and I yanked the cord out of the wall.

"Are you out of your mind?" I demanded. "It's six in the morning. You're going to wake Anthony, not to mention the entire neighborhood."

"Sorry, babe. I'm just trying to get a jump start on some things." This came out as one long jumbled sentence. Sam was sweating and couldn't seem to stand still.

I frowned. "Are you all right? Have you even been to bed?"

"I couldn't sleep. Bad night I guess. I think I'm gonna rearrange some things in here. Hey, how about some coffee? I'll go make us some." Sam talked a mile a minute.

I wondered what he had taken this time.

"Sure," I replied.

I'd do anything to avoid a fight. Living like that frustrated me but agreeing was easier when Sam was in a mood. He could go from happy and animated to violent and scary without warning.

By the time I got downstairs, Sam had coffee going and stood at the stove whisking a pan of eggs. He bounced from subject to subject faster than I could follow.

"I got an email from Maddy," he said. "There's a script she wants me to look at later."

"That's good."

Maddy had been his agent for years. Sam's last few movies had been hit and miss at the box office, with only one being mildly successful. He was aching for a success.

"Yeah, I'm ready to go back to work," he said.

Anthony's voice called for me over the baby monitor, saving me from further conversation. I hopped up before Sam could offer to go. I had a nasty feeling in my gut. Something was coming, but I didn't know what. Once I got Anthony dressed and downstairs, the food sat ready on the table. Sam was hanging up the phone when I walked in.

"Who was that?" I settled Anthony at the table and began fixing his plate.

"That was Vicky. She's in town for the week and wanted to see about you and her getting the kids together."

"Oh yeah? That'd be nice," I said in a neutral voice. "I'll call her back later this afternoon."

I wasn't hungry, but I nibbled while Anthony chowed down.

"Maybe you guys could go have a girl's weekend with the kids?" Sam suggested.

I stared at him, caught off guard. Something was definitely going on. Sam never suggested that I go anywhere. More times than not, if I went somewhere, I had a curfew, and God help me if I didn't get back in time.

"You know," Sam said with a mouthful of food, "if I accept this script, which I probably will, I'll more than likely have a screen test Monday or Tuesday. I'll need time and space to prepare."

I'm sure I looked as dumbfounded as I felt. "Okay? Yeah, if you're sure?"

"Absolutely, you need some time, too."

Sam was giving me permission to go somewhere—and for the entire weekend? *Hell yes.* I quickly called Vicky to make the arrangements. Since Sam was leaving for Maddy's late in the afternoon, I planned on Vicky picking us up around four.

I CLEANED up from breakfast and started my housework. Sam closed himself in his office. I was putting laundry away, carefully arranging Sam's socks in his bottom drawer, when I found the drawer wouldn't close all the way. I tried everything, rearranged the clothes, pulled the drawer open and shut a couple of times, jiggled the drawer. Nothing. Finally, I took the drawer off its track and pulled it out of the dresser.

Feeling around, I retrieved a half-gallon plastic bag with several smaller baggies filled with everything from pot to crystals to fine white powder, a dirty spoon crusted with tarry film, and a syringe.

This was absolutely the last straw. Enraged, I marched down the hall to his office and flung open the door. Startled, Sam looked up with huge eyes.

"What the fuck is this?" I threw the drugs on the floor at his feet.

His gaze snapped from the drugs back to me. "Now, Rosalie, listen—"

"No! I am done with this shit! It's bad enough you come home trashed out of your mind, but you're hiding shit in the house again? You're pathetic."

Sam glowered. "I advise you to stop while you're ahead."

I didn't care anymore. Five years of my life spent on constant fighting, constant begging for my husband to not hurt me. Five years of nothing but hell.

"I'm done, Sam. And I don't care what you do to me. You're pathetic and we are not going to be a part of this anymore. If drugs are the only thing you care about, well, you can have them."

I spun and stalked from the room and headed downstairs, where Anthony watched cartoons. I reached the stairs and strong fingers seized my arm.

Sam swung me around to face him. "*You bitch.* Do you really think you're going to leave me?"

"I know I am. Let me go!"

Despite my terror, rage fueled me. I was leaving. In those few moments in the bedroom, it finally clicked. This was going to be my life forever unless I changed the script.

Sam had been given every chance, every opportunity to fix his mess, and all he had done was piss it all away. He wasn't going to stop, and I damn well wasn't going to be involved. I didn't care if that meant I took Anthony back to Indiana and worked in a drive-thru.

Sam's fingers dug into my arm. "You have nothing without me. I'm not sure what's gotten into your head, but that ends now."

"You're right." I yanked free of his grip.

"I told you, the only way you're leaving me is in a body bag."

Sam spun me facing the stairs, then shoved. I screamed, then bounced off the wall. Pain stabbed my left arm and hip, then I hit on the short landing on my back.

Anthony wailed. I heard his little feet padding toward the

stairs. As long as he stayed in the living room the high banister would hide me from his view. If he reached the bottom of the stairs however, he'd have a full view of the landing where I lay.

"Don't worry, buddy," Sam sing-songed as he descended the stairs to me. "Mommy tripped, but she's okay, aren't you?"

"It's okay, honey. Go watch your show," I called, my voice higher than I intended. I struggled to keep my tone calm and even. I listened, praying I wouldn't hear Anthony begin climbing the stairs.

My arm and shoulder throbbed. Sam grabbed my shirt and pulled my face close to his. "You are not leaving me. Do you understand me?"

"Fuck you," I spat.

Sam hit me upside my head so hard I saw spots. "Keep trying me, Rosalie, and you'll leave in a body bag. Get yourself cleaned up. I have to get my script."

"My arm is broken," I wheezed through the pain.

Sam shrugged. "You should have paid more attention."

I crawled to the banister and pulled myself to my feet. "You pushed me, you sadistic prick."

Sam chuckled, then popped me in the mouth with his fist. "You will respect me. Either that, or I'll beat the respect into you." He leaned close. "You can let go of whatever little ideas you have in your head. I'll see you dead before you see a divorce."

He kissed me, hard, on the lips. Bile rose in my mouth, and all I could think was how I needed to get away from him. So I bit him.

"Goddamn it," Sam roared. He slapped me so hard I tumbled back to the landing. "You love this, don't you?" He dropped to a squat "You love pushing me to the point of hurting you, don't you?"

With each word, Sam battered my shoulders and arms, I wanted to scream from the pain searing through my body. Instead, I bit my tongue and curled into a ball to protect my injured arm and face.

"Don't hit my mommy!" Anthony had quietly climbed the bottom stairs and had seen everything.

"Mommy was bad and needed to be punished, son," Sam said.

Anthony looked from Sam to me. Tears ran down his face, his eyes wide with fright and confusion. Sam hurried down the stairs to him. Scooping him up, Sam hugged him tight. The fear in my son's eyes was more than I could handle. That was all I needed to make my choice. I was leaving.

Sam sat Anthony back down on the stair and patted him on the head. "Daddy has to go for a little bit. Be a good boy and help your mom."

Anthony ran up the stairs to me and collapsed against my chest, his little body shaking with sobs. Sam glared at me, then strode to the door and slammed the front door behind him.

Anthony cried so hard my shirt was soaked in his tears. He took great, gasping gulps of air in as he fought to calm down. I patted his back and whispered to him. My body hummed with pain. I couldn't pinpoint where it hurt more. I just knew that the pain seemed to come from everywhere. My bottom lip felt three sizes too big for my face and I could taste blood. I hadn't realized Sam had busted my lip open. Fighting not to cry and frighten Anthony, I sang him his favorite nursery rhymes until his breathing returned to normal and he stopped shaking.

I eased him back so that I could see his face and said in a soft voice, "Baby. I need you to listen to me. I need you to be a big boy and get me the phone so I can call Uncle Holden."

I gave him a long hug and watched him hurry down the stairs. Seconds later, he returned with the cordless phone. I sent him back downstairs to watch cartoons and dialed Holden. I prayed he was home, but with Vicky being in town I doubted he would be. After the fifth ring, I was about to hang up when he finally answered.

"Holden," was all I could say before I lost what little composure I had. Sobs wracked my body and I couldn't calm down enough to form a single coherent sentence.

Holden said he was on his way and ordered me not to move. After we hung up, I pushed into a sitting position against the wall and cried as quietly as I could. I cried for the last five years of my life, for all the love I'd had for Sam, for all my hopes and dreams. I cried for everything that had turned to shit. I had fought for Sam and our marriage long after he had given up. But now I was done. Threats or no threats, I had to take my baby and leave.

Get those tears out now because you are never crying for that son of a bitch again, a voice in my head ordered.

My sobs had turned to sniffles when Holden come through the front door. "Hey, buddy, where's your mom?" he said. "What happened?"

"Daddy hurt her."

"I'm up here," I called.

"I'm gonna get your mom and then the three of us are leaving, okay?" Holden said. "Grab your shoes for me."

Holden bounded up the stairs two at a time. "Jesus," he whispered when he neared the landing.

"Careful, my arm's broken," I said as he reached me and leaned down to slip an arm beneath my arm.

He eased me up and onto my feet. My left arm hung useless at my side.

"Are you done yet? How much longer?" he demanded.

I clung to him for fear I would fall. "I'm done."

"Do you really mean that?" Hope shone brightly in his eyes.

"Yes. I need you to help me get a few things for this weekend."

"Screw this weekend," he growled. "We need to get you to a doctor."

I shook my head, the regretted the action when pain spiked through my skull. "Clothes first," I said. "I don't know when Sam might be back, and I want to leave before he does. Besides, I promised Anthony we were going to the beach with Vicky and the kids."

"Rosie—"

"Please, help me get out things," I cut in. Despite the agony running rampant through me I needed something to hold onto and I was holding on to my damn plans.

His mouth thinned. "All right."

Holden gently kissed me on the forehead. He helped me get to my feet. I climbed the small set of stairs to my room. Holden followed close behind as I grabbed two changes of clothing each for Anthony and myself.

"Shouldn't we be getting more than this?" Holden said, as he held my overnight bag open for me.

"Things have to look normal." Whatever that was. "I don't want to give Sam a heads up as to what I'm doing until I've filed for divorce."

Anthony had calmed down with Holden's appearance. He'd even gotten his shoes on like Holden asked, although they were on the wrong feet. I scribbled a note for Sam, telling him we were with Vicky, and we left.

.   .   .

ONCE IN THE CAR, my pounding heart began to slow. I didn't know what was going to happen. I just knew that I wasn't going back to Sam.

"Anthony?" Holden said, looking in the rear-view mirror. "I need to take your mom to a doctor. Vicky and the kids are at Poppa Rae's house. I'm going to drop you off, OK?"

"I wanna stay with my mommy," he cried.

My son had seen too much. I wasn't going to force him to stay with Vicky and make the experience worse for him. We went to the urgent care where I could trust the doctor and nurses to not call the cops or the press.

What I feared was a broken arm turned out to be a dislocated shoulder. For a few excruciating seconds, I wished Sam had broken it. I thought I would piss my pants when the doctor pushed the joint back into place.

The old doctor took mercy on me and gave me a pain shot. Along with a script for anti-inflammatories and one for a pain killer. As soon as we left the urgent care Holden went directly to the nearest pharmacy and filled the prescriptions. Holden's silence and rigid driving posture made me nervous.

"What's wrong? You've hardly said anything," I asked.

"Just thinking. Can we talk when we get to Mom and Dad's?"

I tensed. "Yeah."

He put his hand on my leg. By the time we reached the house Anthony had calmed down enough to want to play. Holden took him to the backyard, where we could hear Vicky's kids yelling as they played, then helped me into the house.

Despite the pain shot I was still in agony— *and* woozy at the same time. "Is this going to be bad? What you want to talk about?" I asked.

He shook his head. "Not at all."

My whole body hurt. Holden held on to my good side and opened the door then eased me inside. Louise, Holden's mom, and Vicky looked up from where they sat on the couch. They stopped mid-conversation.

"That bastard!" Vicky spat. "Is your arm broken? Where's Anthony?"

"Dislocated and out back with your two." Holden eased me onto the sofa beside Vicky.

"I'm done. I'm filing for divorce Monday," I said.

"Thank the Lord you've finally seen the light." Vicky threw her hands up.

"Can you guys give us a few minutes?" Holden asked.

"Of course," Louise said.

"Time to check on the monsters anyway." Vicky patted Holden's arm as she and Louise walked past.

Holden sat beside me on the couch. "Rosalie, whatever you need or want to do, I'm here, always."

I choked back a sob. "I don't know what I'm going to do. I don't have any money. The house, my car, the credit cards, everything is in Sam's name. I'm terrified. He's always told me that he'd kill me if I left, and he'd make sure I'd lose Anthony before he kills me."

Holden's mouth thinned. "He can't take Anthony from you. Not with his drug problem and record. There is no judge who's going to give him more than supervised visits. He's never going to touch you again. I won't let that happen. I never should have allowed this to go on this long."

I shook my head. "I'm not your responsibility."

"The hell you're not," he burst out.

"He's crazy," I said. "This isn't over by a long shot. You and I both know that. He is never going to let me leave. Maybe Anthony and I should go to Indiana. You've been saving me since I met you. I can't keep asking that of you."

"You've never asked. Woman, you are the most stubborn female I have ever met in my life." He stood and threw his hands in the air. "Sometimes I think you've got a pair of blinders on." He began to pace.

"Holden...."

He raked his fingers through his hair. "Rosalie, I've done nothing out responsibility or pity. I helped you because I wanted to. I did it because I love you."

"I love you too, Holden, but—"

"Don't do that," he cut me off. "Don't brush me off. I'm in love with you. I always have been."

Tears welled up in my eyes. Deep down, I'd always known what Holden and I had went deeper than friendship, but knowing something and hearing him say it out loud for the first time were two different things.

He sank to his knees in front of me. "You once told me that when the right person would come along. The right person has always been you. I just had to be patient and wait for you to figure that out."

"I don't know what to say."

Holden shook his head. "Don't overthink. I know you feel more for me than just friendship. The way you look at me, the way you kissed me. Don't push me out, not now. Please."

I bit down on my lower lip. My mind swam. The realization that my marriage to Sam was over, that I was really going to leave, slammed into me, and I felt like I was drowning.

"Please, Rosalie, I know you feel this, too," he whispered. "I know there's something there. It's been there since the night I met you. I'm not him, I'm not Sam."

"I know. You could never be him."

"Right now, right here, Rosalie, without the bullshit, without the complications: Do you love me?"

I nodded. "I have for a long time. But I've dragged you

through enough shit, though, and this situation with Sam hasn't even begun. What's coming up is going to top anything that's ever happened before."

"We'll deal with that. All I needed to know was that you love me, too."

Holden kissed me, I jerked from the sharp prick of pain but despite the soreness I kissed him back—gently. I didn't think about what I was doing, didn't question or fight. I let him wash over me. When Holden tried to pull away, I wrapped my good arm around him and pressed my forehead against his.

"Okay then," he breathed, and drew back.

I began to cry.

"I've always loved you," he said.

"What happens now? There's Anthony to think about...."

Holden pressed a kiss on my cheek. "We are not going to worry about that right now. One day at a time."

While that sounded reassuring, I had an awful feeling that something much worse was coming.

Louise poked her head into the room. "I'm sorry to interrupt, but Sam's on the phone, and he insists on speaking with Rosalie."

I could tell by the disgusted look on her face that he was being belligerent and threatening.

Holden stood. "I'll gladly speak to him."

I grabbed his arm. "No, it's better if I talk to him. I don't want to tip him off to anything until I've already filed."

"I really don't think that's a good idea." The panic in Holden's voice told me he was worried that I'd forgive Sam.

But I also knew what Sam would do if he didn't hear from me, and soon. With Holden's help, I hobbled into the kitchen and took the phone.

"Took me long enough to track you down," Sam said.

"You knew I was going with Vicky. You said I could."

"That doesn't mean I don't expect to know where you are."

"Well, now you know," I replied.

"Don't get smart. Holden there?"

"No. I haven't seen him." I hoped my voice wouldn't betray me.

"Uh huh. I figured you'd want to know I'm taking the script. I've got to fly out to New York this Sunday for some screen tests. I should be back Wednesday or Thursday." Sam went silent for a minute. "How bad is the arm?"

"Dislocated. I'll live."

"Shit," he sighed. "I'm sorry, honey. I really don't mean to hurt you. You just make me so damn mad, and you push and push until I do. I'm really sorry."

"Me too," I spat.

"What in the hell is that supposed to mean?" Sam's apologetic voice turned sharp.

Shit! That wasn't what I was going for. "Nothing. I just meant that I'm sorry I push you to do things."

I did my best to sound sincere instead of sarcastic. The silence on the other end of the phone made me question how well I was doing.

"Yeah, well, I expect a phone call letting me know where you are and when you get home."

"I will."

"You damn well better."

"I said I would, Sam."

"Love you," he said.

"Uh huh, bye." I hung up and hoped the last part didn't piss him off too badly.

Most of the time Sam didn't bother to say he loved me anymore, let alone notice if I parroted the phrase. But this situation felt different somehow. I just had a feeling that I couldn't pin down or brush off.

"He's leaving for New York Sunday and won't be back until Wednesday or Thursday," I told Holden and Vicky. "That'll give me enough time to file Monday and pick up things from the house."

"Are you staying here or going back to Indiana?" Vicky asked.

I laughed. "Honestly? I have no idea what I'm doing. Everything is in Sam's name. Indiana is the last place I want to go, though."

"But you are not going back to him, right?" she pressed.

I shook my head. "No. I'm done. I can't allow Anthony to see anything like that ever again."

"We'll figure everything out. Nothing is going to happen to you anymore," Holden said.

"You look like you're in a lot of pain, dear. Didn't the clinic give you anything?" Louise asked.

I nodded. "A pain shot in the office, plus a couple of scripts."

"You can have the anti-inflammatories now and the pain pills in a couple of hours." Holden tore open the package he'd put on the counter, then opened the bottle and handed me two pills.

I'd had enough broken bones to know I didn't like the way pain meds made me feel, but my whole body throbbed. I accepted the glass of water Holden gave me and swallowed the prescription strength Naproxen.

"All right, let's get the kids rounded up and start our weekend." Everyone stared at me, their mouths open. "What? I'm not letting Sam ruin this, too. The kids are looking forward to going, and so am I."

"I'll make you a deal," Holden said. "We stay here tonight

and let you rest. Tomorrow we will go ahead with the plans of taking all the kids to the beach."

I only got as far as opening my mouth before Holden cut me off.

"I'm aware of how your mind works. You going today is your *fuck you* to Sam. However, you're in no condition today. I want you to have a full twenty-four hours of rest and sleep and then I'll take you wherever you want to go."

"What about Anthony?" I asked.

"What about him?" Vicky cocked an eyebrow. "I think we can manage to care for him while you sleep."

"Not another argument," Holden cut in. "I'm going to get the guest bedroom ready and you are going to rest."

"He loves you, you know," Vicky whispered as Holden left the room.

I knew.

THE FOLLOWING morning Holden and Vicky packed up the kids and I and we headed to Santa Barbra. My resolve to continue with the plans Vicky and I had made wavered briefly as my body ached despite the pain killers. One look at my son's smiling face as Holden loaded the car did more for me than the pills. The plan was to simply enjoy the weekend and worry about Sam Monday. We checked into the hotel, then headed for the beach.

I wasn't sure how I was going to explain leaving Sam to Anthony but seeing him so happy and playing with Holden and the other kids, I knew the divorce and the nastiness that was sure to follow were on hold for the moment. I was going to make damn sure he enjoyed this weekend.

For the most part, we were left uninterrupted on the

beach. Every now and then someone would recognize Holden and approach us, but being there was a much needed break from LA. I was sad when we finally had to leave.

AFTER OUR WEEKEND ENDED, Monday brought reality crashing back into view. We left Anthony with Vicky while Holden and I went to speak with his attorney, who got me in that morning with a divorce attorney. We had a half hour meeting with Daniel Morris. He listened as I detailed the hell I had lived with and assured me my nightmare was over. By ten-thirty that morning, I had filed for divorce and a protective order. Holden paid for everything.

I called Joey and asked him to meet Holden and me for a late breakfast. Joey had no idea of what was going on in my marriage outside of Sam's drug use. I had always been too ashamed to tell him. Between Joey's work schedule and my need to hide any evidence of the abuse I suffered I had closed myself off to anyone outside of our circle of knowledge.

"What in the hell happened to you?" he asked when he arrived at the restaurant.

I bit my lip to keep from crying. Holden put an arm around me. It took a few minutes before Joey caught on.

"Did...did Sam do this?" he asked slowly.

Without looking up, I nodded.

"I'll fucking kill him! Where is he?" He glanced around to make sure no one was paying his attention, then returned his attention to me and lifted a brow.

"Sam's in New York," I whispered. "I filed for divorce this morning."

Joey narrowed his eyes. "Is this the first time he's hit you?"

I shifted my eyes away from him.

"Rosalie, is this the first time?"

I shook my head.

"What the hell?" he hissed under his breath. "Why didn't you tell me? Why didn't you leave sooner?"

I couldn't answer him, so Holden gave Joey a short recounting of Sam's violence toward me. Joey sat in silence for a long time.

Finally, he said, "I wish you would've told me. This is why you avoid seeing me so much isn't it? I mean, I knew when you got married and had Anthony things would change. And then when I met Paul and we started dating. I just chalked not seeing each other as often to us both being busy. If I had known you were purposely avoiding me..." Joey's voice grew thicker and thicker until he trailed off.

I couldn't make my eyes meet his.

Over breakfast, Holden went over the plan to get my things from the house and asked Joey if he'd meet us at Holden's storage unit to help unload since I couldn't. Of course, my brother agreed.

I called my parents, but I told them as little as possible, conveying only that if Sam called looking for me, they should tell him they hadn't heard from me. I had to tell my mother a million times that I was fine, and I refused to answer any of her questions, but I'm sure she guessed the truth. Then, we went to my house. After Holden checked it over, he let me go in to start packing the rest of my things.

THE HOUSE FELT EERIE, almost like it was holding an angry breath. The light on the answering machine blinked with twenty-eight messages. I hit play.

"Hey, just checking to see if you made it back okay. Love you," Sam said in his sweet, concerned voice.

Holden snorted. "Like he gives a shit."

"Guess you're not back yet. I'll try again later." His irritated voice.

Several hang ups followed, and finally the one I knew was coming. "I've called everyone and supposedly no one has seen or heard from you. The only other person I can't get a hold of is Holden. You stupid whore. I will find you, and when I do, you are in for a world of hurt. You want to leave? Fine. But you'll leave in a body bag."

Click.

I shivered. This was going to be bad.

Holden wrapped me in a hug. "He's not going to hurt you. Make sure you take that tape as proof of the threats."

I sucked in a deep breath and nodded. "Let's get this over with."

Holden brought in some boxes from his SUV. We'd decided against a moving truck in case someone got nosey and called Sam.

I didn't feel much as I went from room to room, gathering my belongings. This would be the last time I stepped foot inside my home, but I couldn't cry.

I planned to grab our clothes and Anthony's much loved toys, but as I went through the house I found there were items I just couldn't leave behind. Pictures of Anthony, my books, gifts from Holden and my parents over the years. No, these possessions I wouldn't leave. Sam had taken so much from me over the last five years; I damn well wasn't going to let him have it all.

A few hours later, the SUV was packed, and there were just a few more boxes we couldn't fit inside.

"We'll run this over to the storage unit and come back," Holden said.

"You go ahead," I said. "Joey's waiting on you, and I'll finish up here."

Holden frowned. "I don't like the idea of leaving you here alone."

"I know, but there are a few more things, and I need a little time to myself. I need to process the fact that this is the last time I'll ever be in my house."

I wondered if I sounded as defeated as I felt.

Holden sighed. "Okay, I guess. Swear you'll call me if something's not right?"

"Cross my heart."

Holden kissed me on the cheek. "I'll hurry."

Once Holden left, I finally did cry. What I was really doing was saying goodbye. Goodbye to the house I loved so much and goodbye to the life that had died so long ago. When I first moved into the house with Sam, there was so much love and so many dreams. These walls held all the secrets of my life and marriage, the bad and the good.

I chuckled through my tears, remembering my unease when I first moved in. The trip to buy things I liked to make this my house flooded back. I had been so scared of everything back then. Over the years I had done so much redecorating that our house hardly looked like the one I had walked into five years ago.

Sam had done everything he could to ensure we'd be together. He made me feel beautiful and worthy, but he'd slowly ripped all that away through his abuse.

I took my checkbook and bank and credit cards from my purse and laid them neatly on the kitchen table along with my car and house keys and my wedding ring.

I didn't leave a note. I didn't need to. If Sam didn't realize by now that I was leaving, he would when he saw everything on the table. I went upstairs and double checked to ensure I hadn't missed anything.

The phone started ringing as I descended the stairs. The loud, shrill ring echoed until it sounded like the noise was coming from far, far away. I was too busy trying to remember how to breathe to be worried about the phone ringing. Sam stood at the bottom of the stairs.

FOURTEEN

"Honey, I'm home," he sang, then smiled cruelly.

"You're supposed to be in New York," I said.

Sam laughed. "Funny thing about that. I was at the airport and saw this."

He held up a glossy tabloid magazine. Plastered across the cover was a picture of Holden and I on the beach in Santa Barbara, lying on the sand. Holden was leaning over me, stroking my face.

My heart thudded.

Oh my God, oh shit.

"It's a beautiful picture, really," he said in a calm voice. "I also made a couple of phone calls, did a little digging. You filed for divorce this morning."

Sam stood between me and the door. His eyes were bloodshot, and a slick sheen of sweat covered his forehead. He was high. Sometimes, if I just went along with Sam, I'd be able to defuse a situation before it got out of hand, but I doubted I'd be able to this time. Holden would be back soon. Maybe if I could keep Sam talking and moving, I could stall until he got back.

I resisted the urge to take a step backwards. Fear always fed Sam's fury. "Sam...."

"Shut up! How could you do this to me? I've done right by you. You have the best of everything. I risked my career to marry you."

You didn't risk shit, I wanted to say.

"How long have you been fucking him?" he demanded.

"Never, we've never...."

"Goddamn you. Don't lie to me," he roared.

"I'm not, Sam. Nothing's ever happened!"

He bounded up the stairs. I back-peddled half a dozen steps before he reached me. He drew his hand back and slapped me. My head snapped to the side and blood splattered across the white wall. I fell to the hallway carpet, tasting blood.

"Where is my son?" he demanded.

"Indiana," I lied.

This time he drove his fist into my face. My face exploded in pain.

"I know better than that," he said. "Where is he? You can't keep him from me, and even if you did send him to Indiana that's parental kidnapping. Where is he?"

"With my mother."

He punched my cheek. My mouth filled with blood. Spots swam in my vision as Sam lifted me up by my shirt and tossed me down the stairs. I landed on my shoulder and continued all the way to the living room floor where I crumpled against the wall, unable to catch my breath.

"You ungrateful bitch. You want a divorce? You want to leave me and hide my son from me? I don't think so. You don't even have the guts to tell me. You wait until I'm gone and leave behind my back."

"Because of this. I was trying to avoid this," I panted through a fog of pain.

"You never loved me!" Sam screamed.

He was going to kill me. That knowledge had never been clearer than at that moment. "I did!" I managed in a hoarse shout. "Before the drugs and before the abuse."

"You caused this." He half stumbled down the stairs. "If you listened, you wouldn't get hurt. You did this."

Sam was sobbing now. Maybe they were part of his performance, maybe they were real. Either way, his tears didn't matter. They no longer moved me. I didn't care how sorry he was because even if he didn't kill me now, so long as I stayed with him, there would always be a next time.

Sam dropped to his knees on the carpet beside me and grabbed a fistful of my hair. "You can't leave me. I told you that from the beginning, and you agreed. *You promised.*"

"I was sixteen! Please, Sam we—"

"Please?" he bellowed. "Please? You take my son behind my back, pack your things while I'm gone, and you want to ask me please? What kind of person are you? You're the bad guy, here, not me."

He released me and jumped up. He paced, back and forth like a cat, beside me. Catching my breath, I struggled to my knees. My left eye had begun to swell shut. If I could get out the front door, I might have a chance to get help.

Sam talked to himself while he paced. "She promised, she promised, she promised This is on her. Whatever happens, she caused."

I took the opportunity to Army-crawl forward. I had made my way to the couch when he realized what I was doing.

"No, no, no!" he snarled. "Where do you think you're going, Rosalie? We aren't done."

Sam reached me in two long steps and kicked me squarely

in the ribs. Any breath I'd managed to get back expelled on a wave of pain that caused the room to spin. My lungs burned and screamed as bright dots danced before my eyes.

"I told you time and time again, the only way you're leaving me is in a body bag, and since you insist on leaving, that must be what you want."

He stepped over me and strode to the kitchen. I could hear him pulling drawers out, rifling through them. I fought the compulsion to pass out.

With everything I had left, I got to my knees and crawled to the front door. Sam had locked the deadbolt. I would have to stand to reach the lock. Groaning, I pushed myself to my feet and was reaching for the lock when Sam reappeared from the kitchen.

"Where ya going, baby? We're just getting started."

My left eye was now completely swelled shut. I could hardly make Sam out with the other eye. "I'm sorry," I whispered.

Dramatically, Sam cupped his ear with one hand. "I didn't catch that? Did you say you're sorry? Now, you're sorry?"

That was when I saw the knife. If I didn't figure something out quick, I wasn't going to walk out of this house. "Please don't do this, Sam. Even if you don't love me anymore, think of Anthony and what this will do to him."

Sam laughed. "You don't understand, do you? You never have. I love you more than anything. You are the only person I have ever loved. You're mine."

My head spun. "Then let's fix us." That was the only thing I could think to say. As long as it kept me alive, I would have said anything.

Sam shook his head. "No, too late." He grabbed my shirt and pulled me to my feet against him. "You're tainted now. I can smell Holden all over you." Sam backed me against the front door. He kissed my neck, then my face. "I just wish I could be inside you one more time," he whispered.

He kneaded my breast. God, how I wanted to puke. He kept a death grip on the knife with his other hand. I had to think of something.

"You can," I croaked. "Come on, Sam, one more time."

He kissed me hard on the lips, then used the knife to slice open the front of my blouse. I gasped, and he took the noise for encouragement. He pressed the knife to my throat and undid my bra with one hand.

A car door slammed outside, then Holden's hurried footsteps as he shouted my name. Holden pounded on the door.

"Call 911!" I screamed.

"You fucking whore!" Sam raised the knife and slashed.

I jerked aside in time to avoid a stab to the heart. The knife sliced my right arm from shoulder to just past my elbow. I screamed. Blood soaked my shirt sleeve and left a trail as I backed up.

Sam stumbled in my direction, and I kicked him in the nuts as hard as I could. He dropped to the floor, moaning. I lurched toward the kitchen, thinking if I could get out the patio door, I could get to Holden.

I flipped the lock and pulled on the sliding door, but nothing happened. I yanked again, and the door moved maybe half an inch. In my panicked state, I'd forgotten the stopper we used to keep Anthony from opening the door.

Holden must have thought about the patio door at the same time I did because he rounded the corner seconds later. He tried yanking on the door.

"The door's jammed!" I yelled through the glass.

"You're going to pay for that, you cunt!" Sam roared in a hoarse voice from the living room. I couldn't tell if he had gained his feet or not.

Looking around frantically, Holden grabbed a heavy iron patio chair. "Get back!" he shouted.

Holden swung the chair. The glass exploded at the same time Sam grabbed me by my hair and yanked my head back. Cold steel pressed against my neck.

Holden dropped the chair and raised his hands. "Sam, don't hurt her anymore, please."

Sam snickered. "Well, if it isn't lover boy to the rescue."

Hands still raised, Holden stepped over the broken glass and into the kitchen. "Please, let her go," he said.

"You're a bastard, you know that, Holden? Moving in on another man's family. You're my best fucking friend!"

"I'm sorry. Look, the problem is between me and you. Let Rosalie go. This is between us."

"No. She doesn't get off that easy." Sam swayed.

"This is not her fault, Sam," Holden said calmly. "I talked her into everything. I'm the one to blame."

"Holden, don't." I swallowed against the blade.

"Shut up!" Sam shook me. "You love her?" He slashed the knife across my face, just missing my right eye. "Love the whore now." He shoved me toward Holden.

Holden caught me. Sam edged around us and out the broken door. The last thing I remember was Holden cradling me and saying how sorry he was.

I AWOKE IN A HOSPITAL BED, hooked up to several machines and in pain. Holden dozed in a chair next to me. My left eye was swollen shut. I moaned, waking him.

"You're awake," he mumbled sleepily, and smiled as he pushed upright.

My throat was on fire. "What happened? Where is he?" I

twisted my neck, half expecting Sam to be there, ready to finish the job.

Holden grasped my hand and squeezed. He stroked my forehead lightly. "It's ok, Rosalie. Sam's in jail, and you have been granted an emergency order of protection against him. He isn't going to be getting out any time soon."

I nodded, but even that sent a wave of dizziness and pain through my head that forced me to close my good eye for a moment. When I reopened it, I motioned for a drink, and Holden brought me some water.

I drank greedily, then handed him back the cup and collapsed against the pillow. "How bad am I?"

Holden explained my injuries. Three broken ribs. Two black eyes, the one completely shut. Thirty-three stitches to close the gash in my left arm, and twenty-seven on my face.

"I want to see," I said.

Holden shook his head. "No, you don't, honey."

"Yes, I do. Where's my purse?"

He hesitated, then said, "Vicky brought it up, hang on."

"There's a compact somewhere inside," I said.

Silently, Holden dug through my purse and found the mirror. Opening it, he handed it over. My face was three times its normal size, and a jagged line ran from just above my temple past the corner of my eye and down to my chin. The cut was bright, red, and angry. I wept silent tears. That line was going to heal in a cruel, ugly reminder.

"Don't cry, honey," Holden said in a soft voice. "Everything's going to be okay. We'll get through this." He kissed my hand.

"Why would you want to stay? Look at me! He made sure he ruined...."

"Don't," he said sharply. "He didn't ruin a damn thing. You're beautiful, and you always will be. I love you and I've waited all these years for you, so I sure as hell ain't going anywhere now. You're stuck with me."

I tried to smile and failed. My face felt numb and the three sizes larger looked. "Who has Anthony?"

Holden grinned. "He's at my parents' house...with your mom."

"Fuck," I muttered.

"She's beyond pissed. Mainly at me for not telling her what's been going on. I've been ordered to call her as soon as you wake up."

"Not yet," I said. "I'm not ready to deal with her."

Holden held my hand as he recounted what had happened. He'd called 911 as soon as Sam left and told the police everything. They found Sam just outside of our neighborhood and pulled him over.

He was high as a kite. They found various drugs in the car along with the knife he'd used, my blood splattered on it and on Sam. Sam claimed he didn't remember what happened and that he'd never been to the house.

The officers had explained to Holden that Sam had seen the magazine at the airport and decided he wasn't going to New York. He'd gotten a rental car, parked less than half a block from our house, and waited.

How he knew about my filing for divorce we didn't know. The only thing we could figure out was that he must've followed us from Holden's parent's house to the lawyer's office and everywhere else we went that day.

I was so dazed by the enormity of the events of the past few days that I must have zoned out. My mom's voice startled me into the present.

"I thought I told you to call me as soon as she woke up."

"I told him not to." I shifted slightly to better see where my mother stood inside the door, her hands on her hips.

She pointed at Holden. "You're still on my shit list." She crossed the room, pulled up a chair, and got into lecture mode. "Why didn't you tell me?"

"There was no point. I'd made my bed."

"Hell yes, there was point. I am your mother. My job is to protect you. The son of a bitch better be glad he's in jail. All will be better once you and the baby are back home in Indiana."

I looked from her to Holden. "I'm not...I don't know what I'm doing yet."

"You're coming back to Indiana," she said in that voice that didn't allow argument. "There's nothing keeping you here now."

"Stop, please. I don't know what I'm doing yet, and besides, my life is here. Do we have to decide this right now?"

"No, we don't," Holden said quickly.

"Why are you even here?" Mom snapped.

"Because, Janet, I love your daughter. I always have, and I'm not leaving her side."

"Oh yeah?" She snorted. "When did you love her? When he was beating the shit out of her and you did nothing?"

"That's enough!" I yelled. My head began to throb. "Do not do that, Mother. This not his fault. The fault is all mine."

"Look, Jan, I get that you're pissed off and you have every right to be, but I am not the enemy here, okay?" he said. "She's been through a lot, and there's a lot more ahead of her. Right now, we are going to take this one day at a time."

"When does he have court?" I asked.

Holden looked at his watch. "Eleven o'clock. A little less than eight hours from now."

"I have to be there," I said.

"Honey, you don't have to be there. The lawyer is going to

take care of everything. Besides, I don't think you're getting out of here anytime soon," Holden said.

"I don't care. I'll sign out against medical advice. That judge has to see what Sam did to me. He's gotten away with way too much."

"Rosalie..." Holden tried.

"Save it," Mom muttered.

I pushed the call button and argued with the doctor and everyone for another twenty minutes. Everyone got the point when I ripped the IV out of my arm. An hour and a half later, I was pumped full of pain meds and had been given my discharge papers.

No one was happy with me. I didn't really care. When Holden helped me into his parent's living room, Anthony bawled when he saw me, refusing to have anything to do with me. With my mom and Vicky's help, I got dressed for the court hearing, my heart broken.

The press was everywhere. Holden wrapped an arm around me and hustled me inside the courtroom, with my mother close behind.

"Fucking vultures!" he yelled.

With my mom on one side and Holden on the other, I walked slowly toward the front of the courtroom. My lawyer, Daniel Morris, stood at the table in front of the seat on the right side of the room. He looked up from a document he'd been reading and did a double take when he saw me. He practically threw the document on the table and hurried to meet us hallway up the aisle.

"Good God, Rosalie. Holden said you were bad, but my God." He stared.

I rolled my good eye. "Gee, thanks."

His face paled. "I just meant that you should be resting. I've got this handled. You don't have to be here."

"Yes, I do," I said.

"I'm right behind you. I'm right here." Holden squeezed my hand, then he and my mom sat in the front row behind where I sat at the table to Daniel's right.

Sam was brought in handcuffed and shackled. He was still strung out, but I could tell he was coming down. I struggled to my feet as the judge walked in and was seated. Everyone sat back down and Sam strained to look at me. I could see him out of the corner of my eye and did my best to ignore him.

"Rosalie, I'm sorry," he called.

I shuddered. The sudden involuntary movement brought the pain roaring back to life.

The judge banged his gavel. "Mr. Urban, you are not to speak to her again." The judge's eyes shifted to me. "Mrs. Urban, I was under the impression you were hospitalized for your injuries, and from the looks of you that's right where you need to be. You do not have to be here." The pity in his eyes was more than I could stand.

I slowly got to my feet and said, "Your Honor, I have to be here. I've lived this nightmare for five years, and Sam needs to see what he's done. What his addiction has turned him into."

"Rosalie, please, I'll get help," Sam begged.

"One more word, and I'll hold you in contempt, Mr. Urban," the judge half growled.

He returned his attention onto me. I fought not to squirm under his gaze, and I hadn't even done anything wrong. This judge was old school, and he wasn't fucking around.

Finally, he nodded. "I commend you for appearing here today, Mrs. Urban. If at any time you need to leave, you have Mr. Morris let me know and you'll be excused. Now, let's get to the charges."

The charges were numerous: Domestic battery, assault with a deadly weapon, aggravated assault with intent to do bodily harm, driving under the influence, possession of cocaine, and possession of methamphetamine.

"How do you plead, Mr. Urban?" the judge asked.

"My client pleas no contest, your Honor," Sam's attorney replied.

The judge folded his fingers under his chin. Everyone on my side held their breath.

"Mr. Urban, you understand that a no-contest plea is considered to be the same as a guilty plea and that the court will find you guilty on all charges?" he asked.

I turned just enough to see Sam.

"Yes, sir." Sam glared at me.

"Mr. Urban do not look over at her. Don't even breathe in her general direction," the judge warned. "I won't warn you again. Another look, another word and I'll add a charge of intimidation."

I could feel the hate rolling off Sam in waves. Try as I might, I couldn't keep from looking at him.

"All right, and you are making this plea freely and voluntarily and not under coercion or any other misleading terms?" the judge continued.

"Yes, Your Honor," Sam replied.

"Sentencing is scheduled for two weeks from today. You are to be remanded to the Los Angeles County Jail until that time. I'm also granting a lifetime protection order for Mrs. Urban. You are to have absolutely no contact whatsoever with her. Do you understand me, Mr. Urban?"

"Yes, sir."

"That means no phone calls, no letters, and no third-party interactions."

Sam nodded.

"So ordered." The judge banged his gavel.

Holden hurried over to me and carefully hugged me. "It's over, honey. You're free of him."

I wasn't free just yet, but I was pretty damn close. We still had to go before a judge on our divorce. This hearing had only been for the beating and slicing my face. At that moment, the only thing I cared about was getting a pain pill and sleeping. Everything else could wait.

FIFTEEN

THE ROAD to recovery was long. Anthony had no understanding of what had happened. All he knew and understood was that Daddy hurt Mommy, so Daddy went away and now Mommy looked like a monster.

He wouldn't talk about what had happened, nor did he want to hear Sam's name. If Sam was mentioned, Anthony would stick his fingers in his ears and cry. I felt like the worst mother in the world. It was never my intention for Anthony to hate his father.

A few nights after I'd come home from the hospital, Anthony began developing night terrors. My son's tears and shrieks broke my heart, but I knew he was the one suffering.

I wasn't interested in going back to either my house or Indiana, so we moved in with Holden, where both Anthony and I felt safe. Anthony and I started therapy sessions, and over time his night terrors stopped.

Sam was sentenced to fifteen years in prison. Our divorce went through with no problems. I contested nothing and asked for absolutely nothing. There was no prenuptial agreement, and I was entitled to half of everything, but I wanted no reminders of my former life. I had come into my marriage with nothing. I would leave the same way.

A couple of weeks after Sam went to prison, the letters started. His mail was monitored, but he was getting them out to someone, who mailed them to me.

When his letters failed to get a response or reaction, he found a way to call. Sometimes he'd cry and beg for forgiveness, and other times he'd be full of threats. Eventually, we changed our number and the calls stopped.

The first couple of months after the trial were the rockiest. Holden took time away from acting and helped me through the aftermath of leaving Sam. It was a few months into the relationship before we actually had sex, and not once did Holden complain or push.

The first time we made love wasn't planned. We'd had a long week. Anthony was spending time with Holden's parents, and we were on our own for the weekend.

After a day of cleaning and organizing, we laid in bed together watching a movie. Holden was the big spoon, with his arms wrapped around me from behind. As we lay nestled against one another, Holden kissed my neck and moved his arm lightly, grazing my nipple. In night shorts and a tank top with no bra, the friction took me by surprise and my nipple immediately hardened.

"I'm sorry," Holden whispered, his voice husky and strained.

He'd held back for months.

Years, really.

My whole body tingled, and the most pleasant warmth began to spread between my legs. I wanted Holden to touch me everywhere. I wanted to feel him inside me. This moment had been building for years and damn it, it was time.

"Don't be." I could hardly make my voice rise above a

whisper. Instead, I turned so that we were facing each other. Holden's jaw clenched. He'd been so good and patient. I couldn't keep denying him.

Ever so lightly, I kissed him. A tiny moan escaped his lips. I pulled my shirt over my head, breaking away from his hungry mouth only long enough to toss the tank top across the room.

Holden kissed a trail from my neck to my breast. He hovered just above my erect nipple. "Are you sure? Oh! Please be sure," he panted.

I gently put my hand on the back of his head and brought his warm, wet mouth to my breast. I was instantly flooded with warmth and wetness. I had forgotten how good sex could feel. Holden's tongue was so gentle against my skin that I was coming in no time, and he wasn't even inside me yet.

I moaned over and over. "Holden, please...."

He didn't need to be told twice. He moved in between my legs and gently entered me. I was rocked by a massive orgasm as he began to move inside me.

I wrapped my arms and legs around him, bringing him closer to me, and rocked with him. I lost myself in his movements, in the way his skin felt so hot and wet against mine. Holden moaned with each thrust inside me.

I didn't think I could come anymore when one last, leg-shaking orgasm slammed through my body, overtaking Holden at the same time. He pushed into me, moaning my name over and over.

A sleepy, happy smile spread across his face as he stroked my cheek. He seemed reluctant to pull away from me and break the moment. Finally, he slipped from between my legs and snuggled beside me. I laid my head on his chest and allowed him to wrap his arms around me. He played with my hair until we both fell asleep.

Holden had been by my side for years. I knew him like I

knew my favorite book, but the years with Sam had taken a toll on my psyche.

Almost six months into our life without Sam, Anthony began to flourish and became a social butterfly. Gone was the tense and fearful little boy he'd once been. This was both positive and negative. I very much wanted him to be a child while he could. Because my childhood was filled with drunken fights and constant turmoil, I didn't get to be a kid.

The downside was that Anthony never met a stranger. He talked to everyone he saw and that terrified me. The thought of Sam being able to get to Anthony through someone remained a fear I knew I would live with my whole life. If we hadn't had Holden, I'm not sure either of us would have done so well.

Sam's parents sold the house for him and not once did they ever ask to see Anthony or check on him. As far as they were concerned, I put Sam in prison, and from their perspective, if I'd just been a good wife none of this would've happened.

Well, fuck that.

The abuse would've happened no matter what I did because Sam was that type of person. Out of everything, the hardest part to accept was that I allowed his abuse to go on. It had become so commonplace that I simply accepted Sam's violence as normal. Until that day on the stairs, I never realized what the cycle was doing to my child. I convinced myself that the situation was okay because Anthony rarely saw anything happen. He might have heard things behind closed doors, but rarely witnessed Sam hitting me or our arguments getting heated and ugly.

I imagine what he heard was probably far worse in his little mind than what he'd seen, but I didn't realize that at the time. I had failed my child, plain and simple.

How was Anthony supposed to learn hitting wasn't okay if he heard slaps, his father yell, and his mother cry? How was he supposed to know what a healthy, loving marriage was when his parents were anything but that to each other? I had failed my child in every possible way. I damn sure was never going to let that happen again.

I became an activist. I joined my local CODA, Council on Domestic Abuse, and became a spokeswoman. The women I met in the group inspired me. Some had stories twice as bad as mine. I was scared to speak when I first started attending meetings. Most of the women were from working-class families. I felt that because Sam had money, and because I'd have alimony payments, I didn't deserve to be there. I went only to satisfy Holden and my primary doctor, but what started as a chore became a bonding experience like no other. After several meetings where I just sat there, my "sponsor" pulled me aside one night after everyone had left.

"Not talking doesn't do you any good, Rosalie," she said.

I shrugged. "Look, I appreciate you and everyone else here. Most of them already know my story from the gossip magazines. I'm just trying to make my doctor happy, okay? I don't really think I belong here."

"Your husband beat you, didn't he?"

My cheeks grew hot. I shifted my eyes away.

"You belong here as much as anyone else."

"I was able to pick up and just leave. Most of these women left in the middle of the night with the clothes on their backs and no money," I said. "Sally spent two years being beaten and raped by her husband while she squirreled away change from the grocery store so she could leave. I've got the money and means to take care of myself, to protect myself. I don't feel worthy to be in the same room with these women. They have sacrificed so much more than I have."

My sponsor, Darcy narrowed her eyes. "Rosalie, domestic violence is not an economic issue, it isn't a racial issue, and it isn't a religious issue. Domestic violence is an issue in every background. Something that can happen in the wealthiest and Godliest of homes."

Over the next few weeks, I began to understand more about what happened to me and how many people domestic violence affected. As I listened to the other women's stories, I slowly opened up about mine.

My love for Sam had been puppy love built on lust and sex. I did love him, or at least as much as any sixteen-year-old can love someone. I still believe Sam loved me, as well. Eventually, I came to understand that Sam was just as dependent on me as he was on the drugs. His addictive personality would have it no other way.

There were one or two women who resented the fact that I had just been able to pick up and leave, that I hadn't struggled to get away like they had. But as I opened up, they stopped seeing me as the enemy and started seeing me as a fellow survivor.

Shortly thereafter, I became vocal about the abuse women suffered in Hollywood. I was loud, and Hollywood didn't like it. I fought alongside women of every imaginable background for better laws, more resources, and better community support. Holden supported me every step of the way, and my son got to witness what truly a healthy and loving relationship is.

Two years after my divorce from Sam, Holden's parents had Anthony for a weekend of camping and fishing, so Holden and I planned a romantic evening.

We were going out for dinner, so I was upstairs priming and prepping, which took quite a bit longer because of my scar. By 1998 plastic surgery had come a long way, but even with more surgery the scar would have still be very noticeable, so I had decided against the unnecessary pain.

"Woman, we are going to miss our reservation. You're gorgeous. You don't need all that crap on your face anyway," Holden called from the stairs.

"All right, all right," I answered.

I emerged from our bedroom to be greeted by quite a romantic scene. The lights were dimmed, rose petals were strewn across the floor from the top of the stairs down into the dining room. About the time I hit the middle of the stairs, our song "All For Love" began playing. It was the theme song for the 1993 version of *The Three Musketeers*, hands down the best and only version I'll watch.

Giggling, I barely held it together when Holden stepped around the corner to meet me at the bottom of the stairs. He was dressed as Athos, complete with sword.

"What are you doing?" I shook my head, but I was grinning like an idiot.

Holden bowed. "M'lady." He extended a hand.

When I placed my hand in his, he kissed my fingers, then gently danced me through the dining room and into the living room. I nestled my head against his chest and lost myself while Holden hummed along with the song.

"I love you," he said.

There was always such a passion and strength in his voice every single time he said those words.

"I love you, too." All these years later, a simple look or phrase from him still made my heart feel like it might burst from my chest. There were times when I couldn't believe how much I loved Holden.

"This song has always been perfect for us. Eight years you've been in my life. I think I've been your man of good faith, yes?" he asked.

"That and so much more," I whispered .

"Eight years. From the moment you walked into my life, I've never been able to picture being without you. I fell in love with that innocent, scared kid, and found my home in the woman you've been become. I have waited eight long years for this moment."

He dropped to one knee and pulled a ring from his pants pocket. I started at the large square cut emerald set in white gold.

"Marry me, Rosalie?" he whispered.

"Yes, Holden. Yes. I'll marry you."

Through tears, I let him slip the ring onto my finger. When he rose, I threw my arms around his neck. We held each other long after the song had ended.

Eventually we made our way back upstairs, unable to keep our hands off one another. Later, while we were lying on the bed, Holden propped himself up on one elbow and ran a fingertip across my cheek.

"I can't believe you said yes."

I arched a brow. "Were you really that unsure of my answer?"

He shrugged. "A little."

"I love you, Holden. You taught me what it really means to be loved."

"I waited so long for you. You sure were worth the wait."

I kissed him and we wrapped our arms around each other. We fell asleep making plans.

. . .

WE TOOK Holden's parents out to lunch when they returned home and announced our news.

"Good God, it's about time." Sidney, Holden's dad, laughed. "You hear that, Anthony? Holden's going to be your daddy."

Anthony giggled. "He's already my daddy!"

"Indeed, he is," Sidney said, smiling.

This time around my mother was thrilled.

We agreed we did not want an LA wedding, and absolutely no media. We would be married in Indiana.

ON SEPTEMBER 1ST, 1998, Anthony walked me down the aisle and gave me away. Our ceremony was small and intimate, and I got my themed wedding after all, complete with the boys in royal blue and the girls in silver. I wore a gold dress much like the Queen's in *The Three Musketeers*. Anthony was Holden's best man, and my brother Joey and director Dallas Riles stood for him as groomsmen. Vicky served as my maid of honor, and two of my friends from CODA were my bridesmaids.

Holden surprised me with two weeks in Ireland for our honeymoon, and Anthony got to come along.

"I married the both of you, so he gets a honeymoon, too," Holden said.

LIFE WAS TRULY everything I had ever wanted. Holden and I were friends first, before anything else. We knew each other inside and out. There was nothing we wouldn't do for each other.

By the end of 2000, my parents had reconciled, but my

mom was sick. She'd been diagnosed with congestive heart failure and diabetic neuropathy, so Holden bought the house next door to us and moved my parents from Indiana to California. I became her caregiver.

As I adjusted to all the changes, my therapist suggested that I start keeping a journal to better cope. Those journal entries soon turned into short stories. I found an outlet for the way I felt in a safe environment that I was able to control.

Those stories were just for me. I never showed anyone, not my therapist or Holden. They were an easy way for me to explore my anger or sadness without hurting myself or others. My writing went from something I did every once in a while to an everyday routine.

On June 14, 2001, our daughter Shirley Louise Rae made her entrance into the world. She was our honeymoon baby. We had her by planned C-section as Shirley was as stubborn as I am and refused to turn herself or abide by her due date. She had my red hair and fiery temperament and Holden's nose.

A year and a half later, December 21, 2002, Wyatt Michael Rae completed our family. My tubes were cut, tied, and burnt the same day. My life was full, complete, and perfect.

I had never felt more loved. Mom's health held decently, and she had witnessed all three of her grandchildren enter the world. Life just kept moving forward, and Holden and I loved each other through it all.

One afternoon, Holden called to tell me our longtime friend Dallas Riles had a new horror movie he wanted to talk to us about.

"Isn't this like the fourth horror movie he's done lately?" I asked.

"Something like that. Dallas thinks you'd really enjoy it," Holden said.

"Okay, well, invite him over for dinner tonight. I'll run to the store after the kids and I pick Anthony up from school."

"I'll call him back now."

I picked Anthony up, headed to the store, and rushed home to get dinner started. Holden bringing a director or producer home for dinner to discuss a new project wasn't that unusual. We'd hosted Hollywood elites several times over the years.

Holden got home right after the kids and I did and jumped into his routine of helping Anthony with homework and being my second pair of eyes with the babies. Holden took great care to focus only on Anthony to ensure he knew he was every bit as important as Shirley and Wyatt. I had secretly feared Holden would treat Anthony differently, even subconsciously, but he didn't. As far as Holden and his family were concerned, all three of the kids were his, plain and simple.

"What's the movie about?" I asked Holden as I checked on my roast.

"I'm not sure. Horror is all I know."

"You in a horror movie?"

"Hey, I can be scary."

I giggled and rolled my eyes. With homework done, Holden rounded the kids up and took them outside to play. I had everything set and ready to go when Dallas arrived. He'd brought his daughter, Noel, who was a year younger than Anthony. They went to the same school and were best buddies. The kids were thrilled to have someone new to play with.

After dinner, we sent the three older children into the living room while I cuddled Wyatt, soothing him to sleep.

"So, about this movie?" I asked Dallas.

He grinned. "I discovered this amazing writer. I think you're really going to like her. There are some pretty dark parts." Dallas reached into his messenger bag and came out with a script.

"Finally taking in a female's perspective on horror?" I teased, taking the script.

I shifted Wyatt and looked at the title. I jerked my head up from the script and glanced from Dallas to Holden and back. "What the hell? Are you kidding me?"

The title read *Two Evil Eyes* by Rosalie Rae.

My husband and Dallas had the cheesiest grins plastered on their faces.

"How...I don't understand," I stammered.

I was embarrassed and thrilled at the same time. My writing was just for me. I had never shown anyone, not even Holden.

"Holden brought me your story, and I loved it. I just expanded a little to make the story film length," Dallas explained.

Holden got up and took a sleeping Wyatt from my arms and up to his room. I stared in silence at the script. I didn't know what to think. I'd never been good at anything, especially not at the level of writing a movie. Dallas sat quietly with me, allowing me to take everything in. Holden returned and stood behind me, squeezing my shoulders.

"What do you think?" Dallas finally asked.

"I don't know," I said, shaking my head. "I mean, these stories are just bullshit. They're just for fun, a part of my therapy."

"I don't know about the others, but this one is definitely not bullshit. I seriously want to make it into a movie. I want Holden as the star, and I want you on the set as a consultant."

I stared, open mouthed. "You really think I'm that good?"

"Yes, I really do, Rosalie. I wouldn't have taken the time to expand on it and be here just to blow smoke up your ass. The story really is great."

I opened the script and skimmed through. Dallas had changed extraordinarily little, he only took my idea to the next level.

"What do you mean a consultant on the set?" I asked.

"I want you there while we're filming. This is more your vision than mine."

I shook my head. This was a lot to take in.

"You've got to let me make it, Rosalie. You are seriously fucked in the head. That will transfer so amazingly on screen." Dallas winked. I have to admit Dallas had a way of taking the goriest, most sadistic scenarios and transforming them into art on the screen.

"Gee, thanks," I said dryly. "Dallas, I've got Mom and the kids. I have to be at the school to get Anthony every day."

"I promise, you'll have everything you need. We'll set up an area just for the kids, whatever you need. We won't start filming for at least another six months, so we have plenty of time to work everything out."

I pursed my lips in thought. While this all sounded really good, I wasn't convinced, and I was consumed with self-doubt.

"What do you think?" I asked Holden.

"I think you're really going to be kicking yourself if you don't do it."

"I don't know anything about script writing or film making."

"You don't have to," Dallas said quickly. "Leave the details to me. You're just there to advise on the story."

I sighed heavily. Holden and Dallas were making me nervous. They looked like kids on Christmas morning, waiting for the go ahead to open gifts.

"All right, I guess," I agreed. So, I was going to be a writer.

"I'm actually a little ticked at you," I told Holden later that night in bed.

He frowned. "Why?"

"Because those stories weren't meant to see the light of day."

"You have talent, and I love your stories. You do so much for everyone else, you deserve to have something that is yours. And this? This is your thing."

We'll see.

By early 2002, *Two Evil Eyes* was cast and filming started. Dallas gave me everything I needed. I took the kids with me every day and hired a nurse to sit with my mom when I couldn't be there. The movie took nine months to film; we wrapped everything up the last week of September.

On October 4, 2002, my mom passed away peacefully in her home surrounded by my dad, Joey, and my family. Just when we finally had a good relationship, she was gone. I held her hand as she took her last breath.

Mom's death sent me into a deep depression that I struggled through heavily. A month after my mom passed away, my dad had the first of three heart attacks followed by emergency bypass surgery. All his years of drinking had finally caught up to him. It was touch and go for about two months, but he pulled through.

Holden never left my side. I think he cried harder at my mother's funeral than either Joey or I did. Holden and my mom had a special relationship that only they understood. Truthfully, I think she liked Holden more than any of us.

SIXTEEN

MY FATHER's health took a hard turn later that year. He had multiple strokes that left him bedridden. Holden sold Dad's house for him and Dad moved in with us, where I became his full-time caregiver.

At 7:45 on the evening of August 7, 2016, I held my daddy's hand as he turned to me, gave me a smile, and exhaled his final breath.

My father was well loved in our little community. He often did setup and tear down on Dallas's sets so, once news got around, we had a constant stream of calls and visits.

Four days after my father died, we all stood at his and Mom's graves. They lay side-by-side on the large plot where Holden and I would eventually rest to my mother's right.

Shirley, now fifteen, held her younger brother Wyatt and tried to pretend she wasn't crying while Wyatt sobbed. Anthony stood behind them, an ever-present strength his sister and brother often leaned upon, as they did now.

Holden held me close. I shifted my gaze from my father's grave to my mother's and gave her a sad little smile that I knew I'd inherited from her.

"You were right, Mom," I whispered in my mind. *"When I married Sam, I was too young to understand love."*

We seldom spoke of Sam anymore, but I did think of him more often than I should, usually when I caught Anthony staring and I feared the scars on my face were reminding him of his father.

I released a breath. I would never forget Sam. The man I thought he was, or the man he truly was. Thankfully, his face had dimmed in memory. As for the scars inside me...they no longer bleed.

SNEAK PEEK OF JANE DOE
IS MY MOTHER

JANE DOE IS MY MOTHER

MEGAN LEE HEWELL

In British Columbia, in the early months of 1980, a young woman is brutally murdered and buried in a shallow grave. Decades later, two hikers discover her remains on the shore of Cold Lake. In an attempt to identify the girl, authorities recreate her physical appearance in a series of sketches released to the public.

Four hundred kilometers away in the city of Vancouver, one of university professor Nora Devrey's students hands her a newspaper article that features the Jane Doe police sketch. The picture appears to be a pencil drawing of Nora.

Growing up, Nora had known she was adopted at birth but had never been curious about her biological family. Now, she's obsessed with learning as much as she can about her origins and won't stop searching until she discovers Jane Doe's name and any link between herself and the murdered girl.

I graduated from university in 2017 with a BA in Criminology and a vague intention of perhaps applying to law school. I had ambiguous plans for the gap year I planned to take, including writing the LSAT and trying to find an internship with one of the many law firms in Vancouver to gain experience in the field.

That I might find inspiration and write a novel over the course of that year didn't occur to me, at all. During my undergrad career I had taken several creative writing classes for what I considered "easy" credit, and they were easily some of my favorites. It was from these classes that the idea for *Jane Doe* came about in its earliest form. Under the tutelage of my professor in a third-year Crime and Literature class, I began drafting what I imagined to be a monologue performed by an actress on a stage. The character didn't have a name, but her voice outlined a tragic backstory. This was the character who would, at a later time, become Jane Doe. This attempt was a fun (albeit amateur) attempt, and at the end of the semester, the draft went into a box of university notebooks. Then a new semester began, and in the flurry of writing academic papers and quantifying statistics for my degree, Jane Doe's voice was promptly forgotten.

A year later, I was working at a firm in downtown Vancouver, learning about various court processes and legal procedures in efforts to determine if law school truly was what I wanted to pursue. My partner and I had recently relocated to the suburbs outside of the city, and it was during our unpacking that I happened to find the boxes of textbooks and notepads. The chores of organizing and cleaning were set aside for a trip down memory lane. I found that long-abandoned draft of the character I'd created, and the pieces slowly began to fall into place. It was only too easy to weave the narrative of the young woman running to escape the trauma of her past and the tragic consequences of her actions. As her journey took shape in my mind, I began to imagine telling the story of tracing her path, and this led to the creation of Nora Devrey, a character trying to trace the mother she had never known.

It must have been providence that the following day at work I drafted several court documents concerning a plaintiff known only as Jane Doe. The name leapt off the page at me, like the obvious solution to a math equation. I had the stories of Nora Devrey and her biological mother Jane Doe, though I hadn't yet found Jane Doe's real name. The narrative tying the two women together took longer to puzzle out, and the project didn't come to fruition exactly as planned. Along the way, I met characters I hadn't expected, and saw relationships evolve in ways I hadn't imagined. I was able to borrow some elements of Nora's experience from my own life, such as her cozy world in Vancouver and her trips to small towns.

I was aided greatly by my many excursions to the interior of the province of British Columbia. BC has an incredible landscape encompassing almost every terrain—mountains, forests, deserts–and amazing opportunities for hiking both in the provincial parks and in the backcountry. During the summer of 2018 we took every opportunity to escape the city. Several times that summer, we followed the Canyon Route— Highway 97—alongside the Thompson River, sandwiched between looming faces of rock that formed the mountains towering above us. This is the same journey that Malcolm and Nora later follow, and the details are very much unchanged, from the many waterfalls mere meters from their car to the abandoned cemeteries carved into niches of rock.

It is to my partner Jensen, my Malcolm, that the first thanks need to be given. You are a constant positive presence in my life. Your incredible support and unyielding optimism have been invaluable to me during our many years together. I am fortunate to have you and so grateful for you. Thank you for challenging and inspiring me to be the best possible version of myself.

I would also like to thank my sisters Georgie and Freddie, my fellow mischief makers and oldest friends. You have both been so encouraging at every step of the way, and I am lucky that you are my sisters.

To my best friends, Mandy and Breanna, whose presence have made such an incredible difference in my life. You are both so very much appreciated!

As well, to Carolynn, the reason that this journey has been possible. You gave me the courage to dare to dream, and when I faltered, you are the reason I kept trying. Thank you for being my biggest fan and loudest cheerleader, and for shaping this novel into what it became.

And finally, to the staff at Scarsdale who gave me an opportunity and guided me on this amazing and unbelievable journey–Sharona, Kimberly, Stephanie, and Rain. I owe you the deepest debt of gratitude.

I would like to provide the following note: much of what follows reflects real people, places, and events. I have changed names and locations to protect both privacy and reputation. I have also taken liberties with certain facts, turning them into fiction, for the same purpose. Any mistakes are my own, whether through deliberate misinterpretation or accidental omission. I do hope the residents will forgive my lapses.

I would like to dedicate this book to survivors everywhere. We each are faced with obstacles that must be overcome, whether our struggles are well-known or hidden. I honor your struggle and wish you every success in your own journey.

Megan Lee Hewell
    Vancouver, British Columbia
    November 2020

PREFACE

Two major cities dominate the province of British Columbia, Canada: Prince George in the north and Vancouver in the south. Highway 97 connects the two, snaking through hundreds of kilometres of forested mountain range, flat prairieland, low-lying desert, and past the banks of lakes and rivers. This highway provides a lifeline to the small, isolated towns that dot the region.

Jane Doe's story began in one such small town. Lachlan, BC, lies due east of Prince George and directly north of Cold Lake in the Williams Lake Region. A single narrow, dirt-packed road, Chesamore Way, links Lachlan to Highway 97 and to civilization. Lachlan is bordered on three sides by vast stretches of wilderness. It seemed to me, on my first and only visit to the town, that the town sat with its back to a forested wall, observing all who came and went with suspicion.

Before February 2010, I had never heard of Lachlan. Or of Tome, BC. Tome is slightly larger than Lachlan. It sits directly on Hwy 97 and on the banks of Cold Lake. Tome residents trace their ancestry all the way back to the settlers of the Gold Rush, prior to Confederation, and some back even farther still, to a time when the area was inhabited by the Aboriginal and Metis peoples.

Most people who are born in Tome are raised in Tome. They reach adulthood and marry young and start families, and the cycle that began with their parents and grandparents and great-grandparents continues into the new generations. There is little in the town to attract skilled workers or tempt young families to relocate and settle down there. Most who arrive are simply passing through on their way to other destinations. There are few vacationers and even fewer tourists, though the residents of the township will escape on the weekends and travel to Cold Lake for camping, hunting, and fishing.

In short, Tome is an insignificant town that simply exists. Yet for me, it looms large, for this small, tight-knit community is where my story began. Tome is where I was born, abandoned, and found.

Tome is also the town closest to where Jane Doe was found. The clearing where she lay buried for so many years, unknown and entirely forgotten, is several kilometers southwest of the highway, deep in the backwoods of Cold Lake Provincial Park, a hike of two or three hours off a rarely used utility path.

It's safe to say that nothing of great significance ever happened in Tome. Yet in July 2005, the town seemed to be holding its breath.

PROLOGUE

Scott Duggan wanted to escape from Tome, if only for a weekend. His wife, Tina, was pregnant again, and as the first trimester turned into the second, Scott found her to be even more of an unbearable cow. He needed time away from her and his two little brats. So, he convinced his brother Terry to camp out in Cold Lake Provincial Park.

Now Terry wished he'd refused. He gritted his teeth in impatience as he watched Scott try (and fail) to set up the tent. Already, the canvas flap had a large, jagged hole. Scott's foot had gone through it in frustration when he lost his temper with the poles.

It was Terry's tent. It was also Terry's gear, truck, rifle, ammunition, beer, and dog. Scott hadn't really wanted Terry's company, just his stuff. Scott's driver's license had been suspended again—not that the suspension would have stopped him from driving—but his truck was out of gas, and he wouldn't be able to fill it up until next payday unless he siphoned from someone in town.

As Scott was currently unemployed, or "between opportunities," as he liked to say, Terry couldn't be sure when the next payday would come. Scott had already pawned his rifle, and what money had come from that had likely already been squandered. That was why Scott needed Terry's rifle and ammo and beer, and that was why he had wheedled Terry until Terry had agreed. And now, Scott was setting up Terry's tent and using Terry's gear and drinking Terry's beer.

Of course, Scott couldn't borrow all these things without asking Terry to come along.

Terry swigged the lukewarm beverage from the can in his hand. Then he hollered to his dog, Joad, who sniffed about on the far side of the clearing. Joad was barely visible in the shadows of the large cedar trees.

Terry wondered why they weren't setting up the tent in the shade and clenched his jaw even harder. He hollered at the dog again. Joad was snuffing at mole holes and fallen branches and dried grass.

This trip was a last-minute decision. Most likely, Scott stormed out of the house after Tina nagged him about his drinking or his spending habits or his lack of a job. That's why they hadn't made a reservation for a campsite at Cold Lake Provincial Park, and why they had loaded the entire cooler's worth of beer into their backpacks—instead of water, Terry reminded himself—and trekked down the utility path for an hour or two before plunging into the unmapped underbrush during the heat of the day. They hiked for hours around the northern edge of the lake until they were grumpy and sweaty and hungry and tired. Scott's confident assurances that he knew exactly where he was going had turned to grunting and cursing, neither of which did anything to improve Terry's mood, and when they finally collapsed into the clearing at the edge of the lake—an area rife with mosquitoes, no doubt— Terry threw the tent at Scott and snapped that he could put it up himself.

Terry hollered at his dog again. Joad was digging at something in the shade under the cedar trees. The last thing they needed was a disturbed racoon or skunk or some other nocturnal animal to increase the misery of their afternoon.

Already, he was regretting telling Scott to put the tent up himself. Scott was now four beers in, and the alcohol did nothing to improve Scott's proficiency in erecting the tent. Terry winced when the canvas ripped again.

"Stupid fucking poles," Scott growled, and then added with an ugly snarl, "Get your fuckin' dog before he finds a coyote." He pronounced the word "kye-ot," like he'd heard in all the western movies.

"It was your idea to bring him," Terry snapped back, but drained the last of his beer, threw the can into the brush, and stomped across the clearing to where the dog nosed a pile of leaf rot.

At least, it looked like leaf rot from a distance. When Terry got closer, he realized the dog wasn't digging at organic material. He'd found a bit of plastic or rubber, something that didn't break down in the elements. The material might have been blue once, though exposure had weathered it to a dingy gray. Joad mouthed a scrap no larger than Terry's fist, and Terry noticed that another piece lay a few feet away. Whatever it was had been slashed and torn, probably by a wild animal.

"Joad, git!" He swiped at the dog, but Joad continued to paw at whatever he had unearthed.

The gray material was a jacket of some sort, Terry realized, or had been, at some point. It might have once been a windbreaker or a raincoat. Maybe previous campers had left the garment behind in their haste to leave.

Terry slapped at a mosquito. He wanted to go home.

The dog moved to nose a large, smooth rock that lay nearby, bleached white by its exposure to the sun.

"Joad!" He raised his voice and smacked the dog on the side of the head with his open hand.

Joad gave a startled yelp and whined, hopping about, but he didn't scamper away.

Terry wondered at the dog's odd behavior. Then he wondered how the rock had been bleached by the sun and weathered by the elements when it lay protected by the over-arching tree. He reached down and turned over the rock, curious, and jerked his hand away when he saw it for what it was...a human skull.

Get your copy here.

Keep up on our great authors and their books! Join our NEWSLETTER.

www.scarsdalepublishing.com